THE NIGHT RAIDER

THE
NIGHT
RAIDER
and
Other Stories

WALTER D. EDMONDS

LITTLE, BROWN AND COMPANY
BOSTON   TORONTO

FIRST EDITION

"Perfection of Orchard View" originally appeared in the *Saturday Evening Post.*

Library of Congress Cataloging in Publication Data

Edmonds, Walter Dumaux,
    The night raider and other stories.

    CONTENTS: Perfection of Orchard View.—Raging canal.—Charlie Phister's famous bee shot.—The night raider.
    1. New York (State)—Social life and customs—Juvenile literature. 2. New York (State)—Biography—Juvenile literature. [1. New York (State)—Social life and customs] I. Title.
F119.E36   974.7   80–17491
ISBN 0–316–21141–9

DON

*Published simultaneously in Canada
by Little, Brown & Company (Canada) Limited*

PRINTED IN THE UNITED STATES OF AMERICA

For the grandchildren
who have arrived since
They Had a Horse,
with my love

Deborah
Susan
Katharine
Seline
Harriet
Henrietta
Robert
Eleanor

CONTENTS

PERFECTION
OF ORCHARD VIEW

F. SCHEMMERHORN WATKINS of New York City had never had any intention of becoming a gentleman farmer, or even of owning a place in the country. But once in the dim past a great-aunt transferred her entire fortune from the then-infant company of American Telegraph to first farm mortgages in Oneida County, and in due course Schemmerhorn found himself owner of a mortgage on a thousand acres in the Black River Valley.

This had occurred a very short time after two significant events in his life. The first was the sudden jump of his income to five very respectable figures; the second, his marriage in 1908 to Marie Frances Lee. They were both very young and very enthusiastic, and when he discovered that no interest had been paid on the mortgage for the past ten years, they decided to take a week off from New York and investigate.

What they found was a deserted house, from which the last tenant had removed no one knew where, taking the banister of the front staircase away with him.

But the house sat in an open stretch of the valley, the rest of the land was handsomely wooded, and a first-rate creek ran between the buildings. The creek had a splendid site for a dam and it was swimming with trout.

They spent three days examining the property, and when they were through they decided that they had

had a far better time than on their honeymoon in Newport. They had already decided that they wanted to raise a numerous family; the climate seemed ideal for summering children, cool and dry; and the pond they planned for the creek would give Schemmerhorn just the right kind of sport on his weekends.

Before the summer was over they had renovated the house, they had built a small cottage for a caretaker, and they had installed the caretaker himself.

He was an unenthusiastic man by the name of Arnold Meeker, with a hesitation in his speech that amounted almost to complete stoppage. He seemed to regard every suggestion that either one of them made as the most insane foolishness he had ever listened to, but he performed their wishes because he was taking their money.

However, their neighbor, Mr. Ledyard Boyd, had vouched for his honesty, and Marie Watkins thought he was capable of hilling beans, if only one kept after him sufficiently. And besides, he lent a picturesque touch to the place as he went around in his faded overalls and limp felt hat, the curve of his spine a silent, interminable protest.

They even went that fall to the length of buying two Guernsey cows from Mr. Boyd, because it was apparent to Marie Watkins that the first of the numerous family was on its way and they wished to be certain of milk for it in the following spring.

It was in the local train to Utica that Schemmerhorn picked up a farming journal and happened on an advertisement of Berkshire pigs. He showed it to his wife and they immediately fell into a discussion of hams and bacon and little pigs. It developed that they were both devoted to the first two, and that Marie thought the last were the cunningest things in the world. Schemmerhorn pointed out that the first essential of good hams was a first-class, thoroughbred pig. You couldn't get the texture without the proper breeding. No amount of curing and smoking would do that for you. If they were actually going to live in the country, they ought to have the full benefits of the country life. And his wife, as she was accustomed to, agreed with everything he said. By the time they had reached Spuyten Duyvil it was decided that they would go into pigs in a big way. After all, as Mrs. Watkins pointed out, the Armonds raised fancy poultry, and the Boyds horses and Guernsey cattle, so it would make things more interesting if they themselves had a specialty. She began to make a list of the people it would be nice to send a ham to for Christmas. She would get a Virginia recipe; it would be the most original gift.

They found, that winter, that owning a place in the country was a great incentive to social intercourse. When they were alone there were a hundred plans to be decided on; when Marie Watkins entertained her friends, she had a store of anecdotes about rustic help; at his club, Schemmerhorn discovered that a great many of his friends who before had simply bored him with talk of their gardens were really quite interesting when you understood them. But almost none of them was interested in pigs. That, to him, made his own hobby the more fascinating.

And he did not allow it to lapse. From his office almost daily he dictated a letter to Arnold Meeker about what he wanted done at Larchwood, as they had named the place, and early in the winter he took up the subject of pigs. He mentioned that he was going in for Black Berkshires, as they were one of the best breeds for superior hams.

At the beginning of the week, Arnold's usual letter came with laboriously written news of his doings. It was the first of a long series of communications that was to take place over the matter of pigs.

"About hogs, I don't think a Berkshire hog is a very good breed."

"Why don't you?" Schemmerhorn wrote back.

"They ain't so good for fresh pork" — in Arnold's painful fist.

"I am not interested in pork. I want bacon and smoked ham — the best there are."

"I ain't never smoked ham; I don't know how."

"About smoking hams and bacon, we can learn. Mrs. Watkins will get a recipe and we shall work it out together."

> About that smoking business, if Mrs. Watkins wants to do that, it is all right with me. I am being paid by you, and what you want will be all right. Only, a Berkshire hog is not good for pork. For fresh pork, I mean, sir. Mr. Watkins, I don't want for to tell you anything you don't want me to, but that is what we think up here about pork.
>
> Yours truly,
> Arnold Meeker.

Next week, Schemmerhorn finished his investigations, drew a check to a Connecticut breeder, and telegraphed Arnold Meeker:

EXPECT THREE SOWS WEDNESDAY OR THURSDAY STOP
LETTER FOLLOWS

He wrote a long letter describing where he wanted
the sows put for the winter, and enclosing literature
about their feeding and general care, as well as a plan
for a small piggery which he and Marie had worked
out together on the most modern theories, and which
was to be started as soon as possible in the spring.

Arnold's reply came in the Tuesday mail:

Them sows got here all right. They look like
pretty good hogs. I am feeding them the meal and
corn mixed, the way you say, and they look in good
flesh. I got them in the box stall, whare they seem
to like it real good. I hope they make good hams.
I will have them stuck just as soon as I hear from
you; I should think maybe next week, if you can
send me that recipe for smoking them.

Schemmerhorn sprinted for the nearest telegraph
office.

DO NOT STICK THOSE SOWS STOP WAIT FOR LETTER

"Rush it," he said to the puzzled telegraph girl. "It's
very important."

He went back to his office with a black rage clouding
his sight, and his dictated letter set the stenographer's
hand shaking.

"The man's an idiot," he said, aside, to her. "I'd fire
him tomorrow if there was any way of getting someone
else."

His letter ended:

I hope I have made it clear that I want to raise pigs. No matter what you think about it, I am going in for breeding pigs. I got those sows for that purpose. They are valuable stock. So do not slaughter them on any account.

He was still angry when he got home, but his wife laughed.

"I know it would have been terrible, darling, but the idea is too wonderful. He was only trying to be zealous."

"I wish we could get rid of him," said Schemmerhorn.

"I wouldn't get rid of him for worlds!"

Three days later, an unexpected letter arrived from Arnold. He had evidently sat right down to write it; Schemmerhorn could picture him gripping his sad, pale mustache with one hand and licking his pencil, for the writing was alternately very heavy and very light:

I am sorry about sticking those pigs. I thought that was what you bought them for, but your telegram got here all right. I had to pay Bill James $1.50, that being what he gets for sticking three hogs, even if he didn't stick them. It is hard to stick a hog right, so I got him here to do it. We was all glad when your telegram come and we didn't have to go to it. It is hard work dressing three pigs all to once. I have done it once, but it was tiring to me. The sows look fine. We have named them Smut, Ink, and Blackie. They certainly are the blackest hogs you ever see. They are fat. I understand what you mean about using them the way you want. But, Mr. Watkins, if you want little pigs, you will have to get a bore.

Schemmerhorn snorted a good deal about it, but anyway, the sows had been saved, and the sows continued to live and apparently to prosper, for Arnold's next letter said:

It would have been a good time to stick those sows, as we have had real cold and they would have froze well. They look about ready to eat, fat and fine and active. We are well here. Hoping you are the same.

"He sounds as if he were hungry," Mrs. Watkins said.

It was the middle of January when Schemmerhorn heard of the boar. A breeder in Westchester was giving up his farm and clearing off his stock. Among the stock he had some prizewinning Berkshire hogs. These would be auctioned in two weeks, but until that time all stock was open to private bids.

Schemmerhorn looked up the bloodlines, talked it over in his club, and then took Saturday off and went out to see the pigs. As it was rough weather, his wife was unable to go, but the instant he returned, she could tell from his jubilant voice that he had found what he wanted.

"I bought him," he said. "He's a year old, and he's got a fine head and handsome quarters already. His father took first prize in Syracuse, and his grandfather is Grand Champion Berkshire."

He drew a deep breath.

"Was he very expensive?" Mrs. Watkins was thinking of doctors' and nurses' bills, in spite of herself.

"I got him at a real bargain — for six hundred dollars."

"Six hundred dollars! Oh, Schemmerhorn!"

"Never mind," he said. "I'll insure him."

"Can you insure him against Arnold, dear?"

He laughed.

"Anyway, Arnold won't want to stick him. The man warned me about him. He's got rather an ugly temper."

"Tell me all about him."

"Well, he's got a fine, straight back, his head drops well, and his coat is good. He's got white feet."

"I like that," his wife said. "What's his name?"

"Perfection of Orchard View. He's one of the real Perfection Berkshires."

That night he telegraphed:

BOAR BEING SHIPPED EXPRESS FRIDAY

II

On Sunday morning, according to his custom, Arnold Meeker sat down to write his weekly report. He sat at a little walnut desk that Mrs. Watkins had bought especially for him to write at and that did not give him room for his knees, so he had to sit sidewise. He began his letter:

Mr. Watkins.

Dear sir: That hog has came in a good crate. He is a very big piece of a hog. We had quite a job getting him off the car and I had to hire Bill James big sled and team to fetch him over. That will cost you $1.50, because that is what Bill James gets for hauling a hog from Boonville to here. But that hog is a handsome bore all right. But, Mr. Watkins, it surely is a hard hog to handle. He seems to act kind of mean to me right from the start. He got hold of one leg of my new overhaulls, and he still has them. It is good it isn't my leg he got hold of, ha-ha. That overhaull leg will cost you fifty cents (50¢) but I will put it on the bill. Please excuse me now. . . . That was a telegram that just came, and it was from you. It said "has that hog got to Boonville stop I want to know at once stop that hog cost me six hundred dollars stop telegraph immediately." Mr. Watkins, I have telegraphed. I wrote in my telegram "that hog has came and is OK." But what I would like to know is what all those "stops" mean. I would also like to say that I never heard of nobody paying $600 for a hog. That is a lot of money. I could have got those sows bred to a local bore for 75¢ for each, and there would have been just as many pigs, I think, and maybe better pork pigs too. Well, it is as you say.

Mr. Boyd and family has just been here, and they say that surely is some hog and his name is worth $600, but I don't think it is a good name, so I have named him Edward. I always wanted to have a hog named Edward, so I thought you would not mind if I called this one Edward. Only I wanted my hog to be a Chester white. They make nice pork. I mean fresh pork.

Mr. Boyd wants to breed one of his cross-bred Durochs to Edward, so I told him he could for fifty cents (50¢), thinking it would be all right and pay for them overhaulls.

It is very cold here. I am getting in the ice now. The hens ain't laying very good, but I don't think there is anything I can do. Over to Armonds, the hens don't lay either, and I don't expect our hens are as good as theres. The hens is OK.

Hoping you are the same,
Yours truly, your friend,
Arnold Meeker.

He was a little querulous with Mrs. Meeker when he finished that letter, because it was a very long one and took a lot of energy to write. He said to her, "If that feller F.S. ain't crazy, then I am. Paying that money for a hog, and a Berkshire too."

"You get your wages, don't you?" Mrs. Meeker was a trifle sharp. "And we got a home, ain't we, and running water in it? If he wants to put a steeple on his hog house, you hadn't ought to care. It won't hurt for you to make me a decent living."

"It ain't that," said Arnold. "It's this wasting money all the while on telegrams and hogs. A man hadn't ought to do that. If that hog hadn't of came, I could have wrote him, couldn't I? That would have cost him three cents."

He went out dismally to look at Perfection of Orchard View. In his eyes, Perfection was just a big black boar, and he looked up at Arnold with a calculating gleam in his small eyes and wiggled the end of his nose viciously.

"He don't even smell like any hog I ever smelled," Arnold said to himself. "Now, them sows do. Maybe he will after a while."

He brooded for some minutes, turning slowly over in his mind what crazy things a city-bred man can do when turned loose in the country.

But two days later he was sure Mr. Watkins was a loony.

A letter arrived, and among other things, it said:

> Don't offer service to Perfection of Orchard View for less than $25.00. Service down here would cost three times that much. He is one of the most valuable hogs in the country and we can't afford to throw away money like that. I am willing and glad to improve the stock of pigs in Hawkinsville for a reduced fee, but we can never make the farm pay by running it the way you have started.

"Farm!" cried Arnold after he had read this. "Who ever called this a farm, with four hogs, and all of them black, and two cows? He ain't even got a decent team."

He was so stirred that he wrote right back:

> Mr. Watkins.
>
> Dear sir: I let Mr. Boyd have that service on that hog because I was trying to save the farm money. It ain't rightly a farm anyway, but that was what I aimed to do. I seen it covered the expense of my overhaulls getting tore by that Edward pig, so closed before Mr. Boyd could back down. But if you want to charge $25, it is OK with me. You won't make any money at all here that way, though,

because a farmer can usually get his sow served for a dollar at the most. The price of fresh pork is low and it wouldn't pay anybody to pay that much to get a litter of pigs for fresh pork.

Yours truly,

Arnold Meeker.

He thought, as he took the letter down to the post-box by the river, that he could not say any fairer than that, and maybe it would show Mr. Watkins a little sense.

And Mr. Watkins seemed to see his point. He admitted there was sense enough in Arnold's view, but he said he would hold out for twenty-five dollars just the same. Arnold was relieved, because he had not shown his letter to his wife; he had written in the passion of the moment, and he had been in fear of an awkward row and maybe of getting fired. He now told Mrs. Meeker with some pride, but all she said was that if Mr. Watkins wanted to be a fool, it was their business to make it easy for him. Arnold said he wasn't that kind of man, and they quarreled just the same, but anyway he hadn't lost the job.

Perfection of Orchard View, alias Edward, did not seem to miss his sanitary Westchester sty. He took to the old box stall and the swift accumulation of dirty litter like any other hog Arnold had ever seen; he kept in fine flesh and added to it. The cold of February passed, and he smelled to Arnold like an actual hog. March came, and with it a terrible telegram from Mr. Watkins. When he read it, Arnold was stunned. He could not understand it. He thought that Mr. Watkins must be sick. He showed it to his wife. It said:

WEIGH BOAR AS SOON AS POSSIBLE AND TELEGRAPH
WEIGHT TO ME IMMEDIATELY STOP VERY IMPORTANT
STOP AM WRITING

"Where in Crimus am I going to weight that hog?"
he cried. "We ain't got no scales, and he won't sit on no
ordinary hog scales. Not for me. Not Edward. I got to
use a pitchfork now just to look at him."

III

Mr. Schemmerhorn Watkins waited impatiently in
New York, quite unconscious of the disruption of
morale at Larchwood. To him, his request seemed the
most natural thing in the world. Three weeks before,
he had found another member of his club who had
gone in for pigs, and better yet, for Berkshires. They
lunched together every day. They talked bloodlines,
breeding, and, above all, feed. They were both rabid
on the question of feeding.

And after a week it appeared that the friend had
bought a boar named Perfection of Valley View, which
turned out on investigation to be the own brother of
Orchard View, and a hot discussion took place over the
respective merits of the two hogs. Schemmerhorn was
rather keen about it. His friend was a very wealthy
man who had a model farm, and that made him all the
more fanatic about his own little place and his own
man, Arnold Meeker, whom he set up against the other's Iowa hog specialist. Arnold, in Schemmerhorn's
talk, became the peer of any pig man in the country;
Arnold's methods the acme of modern science.

Rivalry between the two became so pronounced that

the whole club caught the spirit of it, and finally, to settle the disputes, it was suggested that the two hogs be weighed and thus prove which method of pig culture was the more successful. That afternoon Schemmerhorn wired.

Next luncheon hour his rival came into the club announcing that Perfection of Valley View weighed five hundred and forty-five pounds.

But Arnold had not sent a word. Schemmerhorn said that his little place was in the backcountry, a fine hog country, to be sure, but it was hard to get over the roads in March. It was probably very cold, too, and Arnold might be waiting for a salubrious day to weigh his hog, as there were no scales on his place.

As a matter of fact, that was what Arnold's letter said:

> We ain't got no scales and I got Mr. Boyds over here. I got Bill James to bring them over with his team. But we couldn't get Edward to set still on them. He bit off the tine on my pitchfork, and then he tried to bite me, but he didn't. He got outside and we had to drive him back into the stall. I don't see no sense in waying that hog anyway. Why do you want it?

Schemmerhorn dictated a long letter. He tried to put a little *esprit de corps* into Arnold.

He explained in detail about the wealthy friend and the wager and the Iowa pig specialist. He finished by asking whether Arnold could not take the hog to Hawkinsville and weigh him on the wagon scales there. Anyway, Arnold could try it.

At the club he had to explain the difficulty. The wealthy man was amused. He said a few days wouldn't make much difference in the weight, and that when Schemmerhorn got the weight, he could reweigh his boar anyway.

Other members who had been making side bets among themselves agreed that that was fair enough. Schemmerhorn had to.

They waited; Schemmerhorn, as patiently as possible. But after two days he wrote another letter, mentioning the wager once more, and even the amount of it, hoping thereby to get a little action.

Arnold's reply came at last:

Mr. Watkins.

Dear sir: When I got your letter I was serprised at you betting one hundred ($100) dollars on a hog, even if it was your own hog. I don't rightly see how you could. I wasn't born in Iowa. But $100 is a lot of money and I will do as much as anyone can to help you win out with it. I forgot to say in my last letter that you owe Bill James $1.50 for bringing the scales over from Boyds. That is what he charges for hauling scales from Boyds to here. I am going to get him here tomorrow morning to haul Edward down to Hawkinsville, whare we will try to way him on the big scales, according to your idea in yours of 8th instant. Then I will let you know what he ways and it will be all over. Hoping you win the bet,

Yours truly, your friend,
Arnold Meeker.

Schemmerhorn did not reply. He waited for the telegram.

It came that evening.

AM WRITING

"My God!" said Schemmerhorn. "What's happened
now?"

Mr. Watkins.

Dear sir: I am sorry if you are disappointed by
what you hear from me now. We have had some
trouble here, along of trying to way that hog,
Edward. I got Bill James over here to haul Edward
over to Hawkinsville, as it was too far to drive
him, and anyway he won't let me get hold of the
ring there is in his nose. He wouldn't let Bill
neither. So we put him in the crate he come in,
and we got him in by giving him a chocolate bar
and putting another inside the crate and shutting
the door with a pole. Those bars will cost you
20¢, 2 @ 10¢ each. I sent Bill James down to
Hawkinsville to buy them, and he got almond
bars, because he thought Edward would like the
ones with nuts in them best, and I guess he was
right. It will cost you one-fifty ($1.50) for Bill
James fetching the chocolate bars from Hawkinsville to here. He took his team and the big sled,
because we still have got some snow. Well, we got
him onto the sled in his crate, and then we went
to Hawkinsville and we dug out the old wagon
scales and we got Edward on it, and they seemed
to work OK, so we took him out of the crate,

because I thought you wanted his naked wate, didn't you?

It was all right, only he didn't like standing there very good. But it was lucky there was a banana wagon near the store — that was the first this year. It has been an awful hard winter with us up here. Because as quick as we let Edward out, he went after my overhaulls again, and since I had them on me, I had to run. But I got there first, ha-ha, and I thought to give him a banana. He liked that. So I give him another, and then I asked the peddler would he sell me a bunch, and he said yes, so I took a bunch, and I walked up to the scales and Edward come real handy. I got him on the scales, and when he wanted to move, I gave him another banana. Well, Bill James, he was going to do the waying, and we had Mr. Bates, the notary, like you said, to look at the balance; only we then discovered that the wates had been lost; nobody having used them scales for some years. I said for God's sake to hurry, as the bananas was almost gone; so Mr. Bates said, "why, don't you balance with anything at all, and then you will have something?" So Bill James, he balanced with some stones, and because the sliding dingus had come off the arm, he had to balance careful. It took nine small stones and seven tenpenny nails and my watch, and then it didn't quite balance; but Mrs. Bates was coming along just then, and she had an egg in her hand that just balanced Edward, which she had found whare one of her hens had stole the nest. So we made a list of them stones, etc, and nails, and I give them to Mr. Bates to keep, him being a notary.

So that is done, thank God, and we had some trouble getting Edward home, because I had sprained my foot getting the bananas and didn't think I could run faster than him to home, he is such an active bore. So I did the best I could, because he wouldn't go into his crate any more, and hired the banana man to come with me, and I rode in the back of his truck and passed Edward a banana whenever he got tired, and so we got him home. I am writing this about the bananas in case it isn't fair in a bet like yours, because he ate two and a half bunches altogether. I had to pay $17.75 for the bananas, and Mr. Bates wants $1.00 for the wate and $1.00 for holding same in safe possession. Bill James gets $1.50 for hauling Edward to Hawkinsville, because that is what he gets for hauling a hog to Hawkinsville from here. But I wouldn't pay him more, though he said it was owing to him thinking he would have to haul Edward home. I saved you $1.50 there, Mr. Watkins, and hope you think that is OK. Trusting this meets your requirements.

Yours truly, your friend,
Arnold Meeker.

P.S.: I have just thought that you don't know how many pounds your hog ways, but I don't either, and I don't know how to find out; if you have any ideas, send them to me and I will follow them as well as I can.

Yours truly, your friend,
Arnold Meeker.

"He just thought," Schemmerhorn said somberly. He looked at his wife and tried to answer her jubilant laughter. But his was wry. He supposed that a woman so near childbirth might act queerly and that she should be humored at all costs.

But he telegraphed:

TAKE HOG TO BOONVILLE TO WEIGH HIM STOP WEIGH
HIM IN CRATE AND AFTER YOU HAVE HIM HOME TAKE
CRATE OVER AND WEIGH IT STOP DEDUCT AND SEND
RESULT STOP TELEGRAPH IMMEDIATELY
WATKINS

IT WILL COST THREE DOLLARS HAULING EDWARD OVER
AND BACK AND SAME FOR CRATE STOP DO YOU WANT
TO SPEND THAT MUCH
MEEKER

YES
WATKINS

EDWARD WONT GO INTO CRATE STOP HE ACTS MEAN
STOP WHAT SHALL I DO
MEEKER

AM WRITING
WATKINS

At first glance, the difficulties had seemed nearly insuperable to Schemmerhorn. But one phrase in Arnold's letter stuck in his mind: "So that is done, thank God." It was indubitably done, and indubitably also, Mr. Bates had the weight of Perfection of Orchard View in safe possession. After considerable heavy thinking, Schemmerhorn thought he saw the way out of their difficulties. So his instructions read:

> "I think you can find out Perfection's weight in pounds as follows: Take the miscellaneous weights now held by Mr. Bates and put them on the pan of the wagon scales in Hawkinsville. Then, with stones or other heavy material on the platform, balance the scales once more. Then take the heavy materials over to Boonville and weigh them. In other words, the heavy materials will represent Perfection."

Schemmerhorn, of course, had been forced to accept Arnold's word that it was impossible to move the boar a second time. And Arnold apparently had welcomed the new solution with relief. After four days of silence, his usual weekly letter came.

> Mr. Watkins.
>
> Dear sir: I was glad you did not want us to try moving that hog any more. I was tired of moving him. So I was glad to do what you said. So we took out the wates. Mr. Bates, as a notary public, said what you said was OK and just and lawful for establishing the hog's wate, so we done it. I had to hire Bill James to haul some stones on his lumber wagon; your carriage team is not heavy enough to draw stones in this awful roads we have got now, with the thaw and all. It will cost you one dollar and 50¢ for Bill James and his team and wagon, that being what he gets for hauling and finding one load of stones. Well, you will want to know

what we wayed up with those stones, and we found Edward wayed 544 pounds; so I guess you lose your bet, which is a shame. But I said I wasn't born in Iowa.

Yours truly, your friend,
Arnold Meeker.

P.S.: I forgot to state that we didn't have the egg with the other weights. We had all the small stones and all the nails, but Mr. Bates couldn't find the egg. I thought maybe that that egg would make a difference, so I borrowed one egg, and it made the difference not quite a pound on the scales, but I think that first egg was a big egg; it looked like almost a goose's egg.

Yours truly,
Arnold Meeker.

Schemmerhorn ground his teeth steadily for twenty minutes. Then, taking command of his temper, he wrote a long and painstaking letter explaining that he had lost the bet by one pound and that something must be done to find that egg.

Arnold replied with unusual promptness:

Mr. Watkins.

Dear sir: In regard that egg. I have see Mr. Bates, and Mrs. Bates says Mr. Bates ate that egg for supper on a baked potatoe. I don't see how I can get it back from whare it is now. Ha-ha. But Mrs. Bates says it was laid by her black hen with the gray feathers in its wings, and she will get another egg from the same hen. Only that hen is always stealing her nest, so it may take some time. I have hired a boy to watch said hen. I think that will be fair, don't you, Mr. Watkins?

> Yours truly, your friend,
> Arnold Meeker.

Schemmerhorn found it difficult to face his club. He went as rarely as possible, and he used for an excuse his wife's advanced condition. It was their first baby, and he quite naturally and truthfully was anxious. But he got no word from Arnold till the following Tuesday.

> Dear sir: That hen of Mrs. Bates is surely contrary and will not lay for anything. I have even bot some Force Feed for her and she has ate a lot, but there is no egg yet. The boy is Ralphy Shane, and he is a bright boy, and I have offered him a dollar when he finds the egg, and he will not miss it as soon as it is laid, you can bet. I don't think black hens is ever good layers. I like white for a color in any animal, horse, hog, hen or human, ha-ha. But do not give up hope. Mrs. Meeker says for to be remembered herewith to Mrs. Watkins, and hopes she is not having a bad time. We have buried three children ourselves, so know how you feel now.
>
> Yours truly, your friend,
> Arnold Meeker.

"The Force Feed is a good idea, and if she doesn't lay, I hope that hen will bust high, wide, and handsome," wrote Schemmerhorn.

> Mr. Watkins,
>   Dear sir: So do I. She is a hell of a hen. But it has been kind of cold here, and maybe she is not

feeling very well. I have talked with Ike Darple, the carpenter, about a hog house for you, and will have it ready for you in the spring. Ike says the plans is very clear and Mrs. Watkins is certainly a clever hand at drawing them. Mrs. Meeker says to thank Mrs. Watkins for all the magazines and papers she is very good to think of sending same when she is so near having a baby, and my wife surely likes to read a lot in winter. I see in the Rural New Yorker whare they have a Chester bore, but he sounds like a good hog just the same. I surely hope that hen lays quick.

Yours truly, your friend,
Arnold Meeker.

Schemmerhorn contained himself in what patience he could. His wife told him she was glad that the pig's weight kept his mind off herself. And at the club they began to lay bets on whether Mrs. Bates's hen would lay an egg or not.

Then came a telegram:

HEN IS DEAD

MEEKER

Schemmerhorn held his head. But half an hour later, just as he was nerving himself to carry the news to the club, a second telegram was handed to him.

HAVE FOUND EGG STOP HAVE WEIGHED ALL WEIGHTS
AND EDWARD WEIGHS 547 POUNDS STOP AM WRITING
STOP IT SURELY IS FINE YOU WIN YOUR BET STOP IT
WAS SOME EGG STOP BATES WITNESSED WEIGHING STOP

ARNOLD

When he went to lunch, he took Arnold's letter with him. It was a long letter and it contained an affidavit made out by Arnold and witnessed and sealed by Reuben Bates, notary public. The document had gained such importance during the month's waiting that it was posted on the club bulletin board.

And Schemmerhorn, with a just sense of pride, pocketed his hundred dollars and went upstairs to the reading room to read Arnold's letter, to write him a forgiving letter full of praise, and to enclose twenty-five of the hundred dollars.

Arnold's letter read:

Mr. Watkins.

Dear sir: That hen surely died. She was out in the Bates garden when Ralphy Shane found her, and she looked kind of crumby, as if she had tried running under one of these road rollers they have on the main highway. Ralphy fetched her in, and then he went out to look some more, because he is a bright boy. He found the egg all right. I believe she must have died of that egg. It was surely a big one. Seeing she was so contrary and nowing we wanted an egg, she wouldn't lay, but that feed I give her must have been working up in her all the while. Well, we put that egg on the beam and then balanced it with flour in a box from the store and then we wayed the flour, and it come to just three pounds. I inclose herewith the paper Mr. Bates made out about it, with my name signed on. I do not know if it was the bananas made the difference in Edward that day, but he surely ate a lot of them.

Well, you are a winner, Mr. Watkins, and you can tell your rich friend that I was not born in Iowa, ha-ha. I was born in Stittville, right in this county. It is a nice town and some day you might like to see it.

I surely hope that Mrs. Watkins is coming through all right. We had a bad time with our first. Mrs. Meeker nearly died of it. We should miss Mrs. Watkins a great lot; she surely has been a good friend to us.

Before I forget it, that makes me think. When do you want them three sows served?

Yours truly, your friend,

Arnold Meeker.

Schemmerhorn sent the word. He telegraphed that night. His telegram said:

MRS. WATKINS BORE A SON LAST NIGHT STOP BOTH
DOING WELL STOP SERVE SOWS AT ONCE

Three days later, he got a long letter from Meeker, the last in the series.

Mr. Watkins.

Dear sir: We are all surely glad to hear your good news and send our best wishes to Mrs. Watkins. It surely is fine to have a son. It will be nice having a little boy round the place, is what Mrs. Meeker says. She wants to know the name and wate of the baby. It surely is fine.

I have had the sows served as you said to, so everything is OK here, as with you. They look fine. It cost $1.50, as I had to get Bill James wagon and team to get them to bore, and that is what he

charges for said service. You also owe the boy
Ralphy Shane, that found that egg, one dollar,
but I have paid it out of the twenty-five you was
so kind as to send me. I appreciate it. If you want
to send me the dollar, it will be OK.

We have got the hog house pretty well built by
now, and it is nice and warm to work and as quick
as we finish the roof, I am going to move the sows
in.

Maybe you will wonder why I had to get Bill
James to take the sows to be served, but I will
tell you. I did not want to tell you before, because
I thought you would be worried by your bet about
Edward's wate and by Mrs. Watkins and all, and
having a baby, and all that business, and your
work. But Edward died the day after I got him
home. He was laying in his stall in the morning,
and I went in and I looked at him, and he didn't
chase me or offer any meanness. He looked sick,
I thought, so I went close, and he rose and bit me
in the foot. I am a little lame, but he died right
after. He just fell over dead. He was surely quite
a bore, I think, and won you a hundred dollars
too.

I did the best I could for him, and cut him
up and dressed him and sold him to Mr. Smith, the
butcher. He gave me two dollars for him. And I
used that to get my shoe mended whare Edward
bit it. He surely took out a piece of the sole, and
it was lucky it was not my foot, too, only a scratch
and pinch, or I would not know how to get my
foot mended. Ha-ha.

That is why I had to take the sows out. I took

them down to Swain's, and the service cost $1.50 for the three of them. That is the price of a service here, 50¢. It surely is lucky it isn't $25.00, isn't it? His bore is a nice one too. A Chester-white Bore that has got some fine big litters round here. He got 20 pigs off Bill Phelps old Duroch sow last year, and Mr. Boyd has had some good luck with him too. So we will have a lot of little pigs this year, and I don't think Edward could have done no better than that. And we will have good fresh pork from them. I know you will be glad about that.

All is fine with us, and hoping that same is with you and Mrs. Watkins,

Your friend,

Arnold Meeker.

RAGING CANAL

❖❖

The prognosticators of the various almanacs had not seen exactly eye to eye about the weather for the first days of April 1833. In the right-hand columns under "Aspects, Holydays, Weather, Remarks, etc.," appeared such divergent offerings as *"Clear Cold,"* *"Pleasant Sunshine,"* or, by one terse authority, *"Gusty."* The Middle States tried to meet all contingencies with *"Showers in Some Places."* A torrential rain was falling.

It had been falling for two days. Tad Brock, the lad who had been doing the research into the almanacs, slopped along in the wake of the two drenched horses in bitter cold. It wasn't his trick rightly. But he knew Lupes McCagg well enough by now to know that he would have to do the two hours of the other driver's trick and then his own, which was six hours, from six o'clock till midnight.

They had had a nasty time an hour back beyond Durhamville. Lupes had fixed the other driver. The boy was green and sickly, and had fallen asleep hanging on to the towrope. The team had stopped, naturally; the boy had slid back along the towrope into the canal, and the boat with lost way was nearly blown aground.

Lupes had got the team going in the nick of time, snubbed the boat to the towpath; and then he had gone back, wading, to fish up the boy. He'd found him in the water, half-drowned, had thrown him on the boat and brought him to, and had then flogged him. Lupes was known from one end of the canal to the other as a bad man to work for.

Tad, finishing his sleep in the stable with his own team, had been waked by the boy's yelling. The yells hadn't lasted long. By the time the steersman, Casper, had come to the stable and hauled Tad out, the boy was lying on the deck with his shirt torn and bloody and his face like salt pork in the falling rain.

Lupes stood a little way away from him with his rawhide still in his fist. He hadn't even bothered to put his coat on. His wet pants stuck tight around his heavy legs, and his thick hair and beard caught the rain. He didn't seem to see Tad at all but stood rumbling to himself, and now and then he glanced at the small body of the driver boy and growled something about learning him, and breaking-in. When Casper asked in a scared way, "Did you kill him, Lupes?" McCagg just went on rumbling.

Casper said to Tad, "You get out there and drive Billy's trick out. I'm steering."

Tad looked away from Billy. The boy had only been on the boat for three days. Probably some crazy little emigrant run away from his family. Going to make his fortune on the Grand Canal. None of them knew anything about him. He hadn't any warm clothes and only a light pair of shoes. But now he wasn't shivering, anyway.

Tad drove about half an hour before he heard anything from the boat. Then it was Casper letting out a couple of toots on the horn, and Tad stood still and let the boat come up to him through the rain.

It was getting dark, and Casper had lit the bow lantern, and the light from the cabin showed him standing about as wet and miserable as Tad was himself, with a steady drip of rain falling off the end of his thin nose.

"Know that hay barn up ahead, Tad?"

"Yeah."

"Lupes says for you to stop when you come up to it. But if there's any boats around, you keep on hauling, see?"

"Yeah."

Tad had to pound up through the mud to overhaul the straining team. There was still frost coming out of the clay and the footing was bad for the horses. They were already slacking up. Even in three days of Billy's driving, they'd got into bad habits. Tad unlimbered his whip and started popping it. He didn't beat the horses the way some drivers did, but he popped the whip and let them have the snapper here and there, just for a touch. The way he had learned to handle a snake whip was just about all he had learned on the Erie, but he had learned that so well that even Lupes was getting careful the way he treated him.

Lupes had got Tad out of an orphanage in Albany; papers made over and the whole thing legal until Tad would be twenty-one. That was the only reason Tad had stuck to the boat so long. He had tried to run away the first year, but a sheriff had got him in Fayetteville and returned him to the *Western Belle*. What Lupes had done that night had fixed Tad on the boat for three years now. He'd been tougher than Billy, that was all. He had been tougher than half a dozen other boys. Some had run away at the next port they were able to walk at and because they weren't legally bound to Lupes he hadn't been able to put the sheriff onto them. But a couple of boys had been left ashore the way Billy was going to be. Tad knew what that meant.

They reached the barn just about dark and as there weren't any boats, except one they had just passed going west, Tad stopped the horses.

Lupes came on deck and picked Billy off the planks. He said, "You and Casp get out your own team."

"It ain't time for my horses," Tad said.

"You'll have to change them in an hour. This'll save time." Lupes stood holding the boy over one arm. "You'll God-damned do it anyway, see."

He walked towards Tad along the side deck and came down the horse bridge Casper had run on shore. "If anybody comes along, Casp, we're changing teams. If anyone says where's Lupes you tell him to go to hell."

Tad said, "I'll tell him you've gone back of the barn to —"

"You'll keep your dirty mouth shut."

Casper was looking scared when they got out the new horses.

"We got to do what he says. Anybody would say we was party to it. *He*'d say so. They'd believe Lupes."

It was perfectly true. When Lupes put on his Sunday suit and combed his brown hair and beard, he was a fine, respectable-looking man. He'd tell a Mission worker, "Well, maybe I do give my boys a licking. But you know yourself what they're like. Always smoking and getting after the gin. They got to be handled up a little, Mister," and the missionary would believe him.

Tad saw Lupes break the hasp on the hay-barn door and go into the black opening. He carried Billy a good deal the way a bear would handle a spring lamb.

Tad said, "I don't see why you stick it out with him, Casp."

Casper said, "He don't bother me. He feeds decent. Anyway he ain't bad till he gets a mad on. Then I couldn't stop him if I wanted to."

That was true enough. There probably wasn't a man on the canal could stop Lupes. He hadn't been whipped in all the time Tad had been on the *Western Belle*. It made a man like Casper a little proud in spite of everything to be known for a *Western Belle* man.

Lupes stood five feet ten and weighed about two hundred. There were plenty of men bigger, but there weren't many so powerful. The only man he hadn't tied up against was a new boatman from Troy. They said he was a Swedish emigrant and the biggest man anybody had seen on the ditch in a long while. His name was Johnson and he was running a boat for the Troy and Oswego Company. Those were yellow boats.

Tad got the new team linked to the eveners and took the lantern Casper handed him. Once the horses had way up he would hang the bail to a hook on the eveners. It gave the steersman a line on the towpath bank.

The door of the barn banged shut and the rain started coming down harder. There was no wind. Just the rain fell harder. It came pretty near straight down, and the horses started shivering their withers.

Lupes McCagg came back across the meadow and heaved the horse bridge on board. He took a running jump and caught the cat rail and climbed the side bolt-heads with his toes.

"Get going," he yelled at Tad. "Get going, you God-damned lousy little crumb."

He waited till the horses had the boat moving and said to the steersman, "Ain't no sense in being seen stopped here even if we was changing teams."

"That's right, Lupes."

The boat went ahead in little jerks, caught way gradually, as Casper eased it out from the bank.

"Ain't anyone seen anything, I calculate," he said.

"Seen what?" Lupes whirled and looked so threaten-ing that Casper almost stepped back off the boat.

"Nothing, Lupes. Honest to God. I was just talking. Funny what a man will say."

Lupes grumbled something and went down into the cabin.

Casper could see him through the window changing his wet clothes. Then, when he was all through and had chucked another chunk of wood in the stove, Lupes sat down and started dealing himself a solitaire game.

Up ahead behind the horses Tad wondered where Lupes had put Billy down. The rain kept finding a way inside his shirt and trickles of it worked down his wishbone, coming up against his belt over his inwards. Wet and cold like that made a man feel sickish. It made him feel lonesome, hung out of the world on the wrong end of a towline.

He hooked his lantern on to the eveners and put his hands into his pockets and hunched his shoulders so the wet front of his shirt wouldn't keep drawing on his belly. The line of the water's edge kept moving slowly back through the light, showing the dead winter grass lying on the water, and the rain falling on it, and old cattails standing up, their heads broken by the spring towlines. There weren't even any peepers going a night like this.

But off to the right there were lights; two yellow windows, of a farmhouse, and a dog that barked. The dog sounded as if he was barking from under a porch, but then he came out from it and must have got on the stoop because he started howling. It wasn't a loud howl — kind of a please-let-me-inside howl. The door opened and a man came out in his pants and under-shirt and shouted something at the dog, but a woman came out after him. She was in her petticoat and Tad figured they were just about getting ready to go to bed. They were too far away for him to see if the woman was pretty or not, or if she was young. But he marked the place so he could keep an eye out for her the next time they hauled this part of the long level in daylight. It would make a difference to him if she was pretty. He could think of her like that getting ready to go to bed with a man.

He had things all along the canal he could remember. They gave him something to think about, when he was doing his trick. All sorts of people. He had seen a packet boat on a bend and a man in a high hat and a lady in a straw bonnet who had been walking a short cut. They couldn't be seen from the packet boat, because there were trees between. The man had his arms around the girl, and her bonnet was hanging on the back of her shoulders from two ribbons, and the man was kissing her as if he was going to break her over his arms and she was kissing him back. Then, coming through Bushnell's Basin one July morning, when he was driving on the other trick, about three o'clock he saw a horse and a buggy in front of a farmhouse. There was a light in the window upstairs and because the house was a little low down he could just see in. He saw a bed and a woman in it, and a man in a nightshirt crying, and a doctor holding a baby. There was another woman in the room; she was standing just beside the window, and the other people couldn't see her, but Tad could. She was having a drink from a small bottle. But for weeks he wondered if the woman in the bed was dead. Then one day they stopped near Bushnell's for a dozen barrels of apples on a mixed load and he went by the house and saw a baby on the porch and a young woman — not more than a girl, not hardly older than he was — tending it. He asked her for a drink of water, but she gave him cider. But even then he didn't have the nerve to ask her if she was the mother of the baby.

Across the canal, in the farmhouse door, the woman was letting the dog into the house, and the door shut, and Tad remembered that it was early for people to go to bed. It wasn't but a little past six, even if it was dark.

He thought there was a bridge coming, so he looked for it. Then he saw it, and a team and a boat were just coming through it.

The bow lantern of the other boat showed it yellow. It had a brown trim. Tad knew it was a Troy and Oswego boat.

"Bridge!" he yelled for Casper.

Casper tooted on his horn, a long one for the bridge and then he saw the boat and tooted again, three toots. The other boat tooted back three toots. That meant the other boat wanted the *Western Belle* to make over the way she ought to.

Tad heard Casper yelling down to Lupes and he let his team go on, wondering if he hadn't ought to stop them. But Lupes didn't get over on a lonely stretch for another boat. If they didn't either, they would have to fight.

Lupes came on deck and roared, "You keep them horses right on going, Tad."

Then he took one jump and hit the towpath and came running after the team. He went right by Tad and Tad yelled, "It's a Troy and Oswego."

"By God."

Lupes was ahead now. He caught the heads of the other boat's team and swung them off the towpath and unhooked the towline and took that with him so they couldn't do any good by keeping going.

When he dropped it, the driver boy came after it and picked it up. Lupes knocked him down with the back of his hand. The boy went down so hard he stayed and Tad realized he wouldn't have to fight him. He was glad of it. He didn't feel like fighting more than one driver boy.

Lupes was now beside the other boat and bawling fit to kill a goat. The man on the other boat was bawling back so they couldn't hear each other.

"I don't get out of the way for any boat," yelled Lupes.

"Who the hell are you?"

"Lupes McCagg on the *Western Belle.*"

"Yas? Well, I don't get out the way either. Boats coming east has to on this level."

"Who the hell are you?"

"I'm Johnson."

"Did your mother call you that?"

"By God."

Tad yelped at Casper, "Tie her up. There's a fence with good posts and they'll hold her here."

He and Casper snubbed the boat and Casper came ashore and they went up to see what was going on. Casper had the end of a boat hook. Tad kicked the boy a little but the boy didn't want to fight. He was crying. "He broke my jaw. I can feel it. It hurts."

Then the boy got up behind them, still holding his jaw, and came along to see his boatman lick the boatman that had knocked his jaw.

The yellow boat had snubbed to the bridge timbers and was lying under the bridge, with her bow lantern making plenty of light. Tad and Casper got under the bridge out of the rain. Tad saw the second driver boy looking out of the stable hatch.

Tad said, "Want a fight?"

The boy ducked back. Tad thought contemptuously that Johnson didn't have much in the way of boat hands. He watched the steersman come up in his undershirt and hat and then go back for coat and shoes. The other steersman saw that he'd have to handle a steersman and a driver and Tad looked big to him.

"That makes it even," Tad said to Casper. "Let's sit down."

"By God," said Casper. "Look at the size of him."

Tad said wonderingly, "I thought Swedes was light."

"I guess it don't make much difference."

The Swede was colossal; when he got down on the towpath and confronted Lupes McCagg, he stood with his chin opposite the other's eyes. He was clean shaven but he had thick black hair and his bare arms were furred like a black bear. He must have weighed near two hundred and fifty pounds. The only thing the matter with him was that he was slow.

Lupes McCagg never gave him a chance. He hit him in the middle before the man could drop his fists and hit him on the chin when he reached out. Lupes was what he called an inside puncher. He hit straight out from his barrel chest, but the Swede worked like a windmill. And fighting under the low timbers of the bridge he kept pulling his head down for fear of hitting it. Every time he did, Lupes got a clear shot. In about five minutes the Swede's face looked like a bad tomato. Blood was running down his cheeks and over his mouth, and when he blew out his breath he sprayed the blood over Lupes's face.

"Jeepers," Tad said to Casper. "Why don't he go down?"

"It's his feet," said Casper. "Look at them, will you?"

The Swede moved ponderously on them, in short steps, back and forth. He was like some kind of dull ox, turning just enough to keep his face to danger. He dripped blood and he swallowed it, but Lupes did not let up. He didn't say, "Got enough?" He was savage, wanting to lay the man out. Tad thought maybe it was because of Billy, and that Lupes felt if he could fell this big brute he would forget what he had done to the boy. But he knew Lupes would forget anyway. He was just savage.

He kept boring in on the great body in front of him, picking his shots, and all of a sudden he said, "You big crumb, I'm going to knock your teeth down." And he did. The Swede spat them out and rubbed his face with the back of one fist and looked sick. Lupes got him in the middle and the Swede made the first sound he had outside of breathing since the fight started. He made a sort of moaning sound, so even Casper felt sorry for him. The men and the two boys of the other boat were staring as if they just couldn't believe it.

Then the Swede pulled a punch somewhere out of the dark and it caught Lupes on the side of the head so that his head snapped almost onto the other shoulder. It was a blow. It knocked the senses clean out of Lupes for a minute and he stood there rocking up and down with his knees. But the Swede was so blind whipped he could not lift his hands again, and Lupes came to and finished him.

It was the bloodiest finish Tad ever hoped to see. When it was over, the other boat crew lugged the man on board and got their boat meekly over to the far shore, and they were so stunned they forgot the towline had been unhooked and one of the boys had to wade back with it, fishing it out of the canal bottom as he came along. He was half-bogged when the *Western Belle* pulled through.

Lupes McCagg went into the cabin and washed his face and put brine on his fists and came back on deck.

"We'll stop when we come to Rose Tavern," he yelled at Tad. "I want a drink."

"That surely was a fight," Casper said to him. "You surely ringed him."

Lupes growled at him. "I guess he ain't going to set himself up as no bully yet."

"He never had no chance," said Casper. "My, my!"

The rain hadn't stopped, but the wind had started to blow and that made it worse. Tad hunched along behind his horses. He didn't have to pay much attention to them. They were a new team, pretty near a thousand apiece, about the heaviest horses he had ever driven, and they were still fat and strong and willing to pull. They were both blacks. He took pride in them and spent more time than he did on most horses cleaning them up after their trick.

But he was bitter now. He was bitter about McCagg. He had always hoped, ever since they'd heard of Johnson, that the Swede would lick McCagg. He wanted to see somebody who could lick McCagg till he couldn't move — till McCagg lay on the ground the way Billy had laid on the boat, or the way Tad himself had laid the time McCagg fixed him after the sheriff brought him back.

Tad remembered that time. The sheriff had picked him up in Fayetteville standing right on the main road. Tad was only fourteen then and he'd thought, being he was away from the canal, that nobody could do anything to him. Of course he had had no money except fifty cents he'd found in under the Genesee Street bridge in Utica three months before. With that he'd bought himself a knife. He was hungry and he was looking for work. He saw a man sitting on his front stoop reading a paper. To Tad he looked like an easy-

going man, and he said, "You want work, hey, son?"
He grinned at Tad, and he said, "Well, I might find
some work for a boy — doing chores. You split kin-
dling for my woman?"

"Yes," said Tad. He was ready to do anything.

"Well, you can go around back and split some and
then split some of that corded wood and maybe you
can have dinner with us."

Tad went to work for an hour and pretty soon the
man came back and said, "You work fast. How old are
you, son?"

Tad said he was fourteen.

"That's good work for a boy your age. What's your
name?"

Tad said, "Tad Brock."

The man grunted and said he was glad to know and
Tad had better come in and eat. He did. He ate so
much the man said, "I guess you hain't had a good
meal in some time. Where you come from?"

Tad said he'd been working on the canal. He didn't
feel worried. The man looked so easygoing and praised
him up so. He asked Tad where his parents lived, and
Tad said he was an orphan, and when the man asked,
he said he'd come from a place in Albany. It was the
first time he had ever got praised for work and he was
anxious to do everything the man wanted because he
thought maybe he could get a permanent job. Of
course he didn't realize the man was a sheriff.

He didn't even realize when the man said a couple
of days later that he had to go to Syracuse and see a
man on business and for Tad to come along to mind
the horse. Tad was pleased to go, and the man let him

drive. He went into a saloon a couple of blocks off the canal and stayed half an hour. When he came out, he got into the wagon beside Tad and said, "My friend's coming out now. We'll just set here and tell him good-bye."

The friend came out and it was Lupes McCagg. He said, "Why hello, Tad." He was dressed in his best clothes and looked like a fine decent citizen. "I hope you've had a nice visit with my friend McCarthy," Lupes said. "I hope he was a good boy, McCarthy."

McCarthy grinned easy and said Tad had been useful — praised him about the wood he had split and all that and said he was sorry to see him go. Then Lupes said, well, him and Tad would have to go back. "Tad's a good worker, Sheriff," he said. "I can't get along without Tad."

Both the men started laughing then, and Lupes said, "Get down." Tad got down. He saw he'd been fooled and he knew what was coming to him. He knew he couldn't do anything. Nobody would believe him. He went with Lupes and Lupes kept saying how nice it would be to get back to the boat. "I bet you been looking forward to coming back. What did you say?" he asked. "Well, you surely gave us a laugh."

Tad went along shivering in his bare feet, though it was a hot sun. He was small and skinny then. Lupes even took him into a saloon and had a drink and said how he had got his best driver boy back from a trip. He took off his hat to a missionary on the street. He looked nice and handsome as a man could look. You would have thought he was a deacon.

He drew out that walk to the boat, talking all the

time, with Tad barely able to walk beside him. They went on board and they went down into the cabin and Lupes shut the door and opened the slide door into the bottom of the pit and told Tad to go into that.

"See if she's leaking," he said.

Tad went and said the boat wasn't leaking more than usual.

"Keep an eye on it till dark," said Lupes, "then we'll let you out." Tad sat there on a crate watching the sky through the cracks in the pit hatches until the sky got dark. He heard the water going by and the rats picking up loose grain and heard boats passing them, horns and people talking, and horses getting the whip, and he thought about what Lupes was going to do to him.

Once, Casper came to the slide and said, "By God you was a fool," and went away.

Then the tricks changed and Lupes came down into the cabin and cooked his supper and drank some gin and smoked a stogie. The smell of it came through the cracks and hung around Tad, and he felt he was getting sick. When he saw Lupes open the door he was sick and Lupes got him a basin of water and told him to wash himself. When he had done that and come out Lupes said, "That's better, I couldn't whip a boy messed up like you was." He stood a minute looking Tad over. He said, "Would you rather lay down on the table or would you rather lay down on deck. You can take your time, because it ain't going to make much difference. We got five hours left."

Tad remembered himself a little skinny boy reaching for the knife he had bought. He must have looked like a rat. He pulled the knife and made a pass with it but he didn't even get to Lupes. He felt the butt end of the whip knock his wrist and he yelled. He could remember that yell now, because with it he saw Lupes's face go mad. Lupes laid him over the table and flogged him.

When he came to, he was back among the crates in the pit and a couple of rats were taking loose pieces of his shirt for nests. Casper saved his life, stealing some of Lupes's fist brine and putting it over his raw back. Casper slipped him some food too, later. He dropped it on the floor accidental-like near the slide door and Tad could get it from there.

But after that Lupes never gave him a chance to get away. He had the papers to bring Tad back. He said, if Tad didn't believe it, he could try again.

"You got to have money to get away," Casper explained. "Lupes had to pay money to get you back and you'd have to have more money to buy off sheriffs and such."

But Tad was a bound-out orphan and couldn't get any wages.

Altogether he had only about five dollars saved up here and there even now. He carried it in a pouch on the inside of his trouser band. He had seen the piece in the paper that Lupes had had written the time he went away. "Ten dollars reward," it said. He couldn't safely run away till he had ten dollars. But he was about sick of Lupes, even though Lupes wasn't so bad now since Tad had learned to handle a whip. He had seen Tad lay open a man's face in one of the fights for a lock. Lupes didn't want his face hurt. He hardly had a scar on it in spite of all his fights.

Tad wished to God the Swede had found that one punch before he was too blind to follow it up. But wishing to God never helped a boy driving the canal. He thought maybe he could get out of the rain for a spell when they got to Rose Tavern.

Rose Tavern was a long white house about a mile east of Durhamville. It stood in a grove of maples fifty yards from the towpath. It didn't show much light, but boaters knew where it was by the row of snubbing posts set in along the towpath.

The bar was in a room that had two fireplaces with mantels of black cherry, and the room paneled with it. The rail of the staircase was genuine mahogany but the spindles were birch and painted. Mrs. Andrews told Tad that. The spindles got broke so regular it didn't pay to have them of good wood. The house had been built by a French Lord, she said, a Duke or a Count or something who had come over when most of the rest of the French nobility were having their heads cut off. But he'd lost his money or something, anyway he'd left, and when the canal was dug through so close to the place, the people who had bought it from him tried to sell it because they were afraid they could not keep their children from being kidnapped by canallers. Mrs. Andrews had got the place cheap.

There were eleven bedrooms in it so she boarded canallers in winter, and Lupes always managed to end the season close by and was one of her regular customers. He hired Tad out to Mrs. Andrews for a chore boy in the winters, to split wood and tend the fires. That paid for Tad's board and some of Lupes's also. Most of the time Lupes left Tad alone. He was working for Mrs. Andrews and it was up to her to lick him if he didn't do the work. But Tad got along fine with Mrs. Andrews.

The lights hardly showed through the maple trees and lilac bushes, but Tad knew it easy enough and yelled to Casper they were coming to Rose Tavern. He stopped the horses and ran back to get the snubbing ropes and tie in the *Western Belle*. Then he went back for the horses and brought them opposite the bow of the boat to put them on board. It was raining hard.

Lupes came on deck and asked him what the hell he thought he was doing. Tad said he was going to put the horses on board. Lupes said they could stay outside. "I'm only going to get a couple of quick ones."

"They're hot," Tad said. "And they're green horses."

"I said they could stay out here," Lupes said. "I don't want to be delayed, see." He talked pretty quietly, but he walked down the plank and up to Tad and looked at him in the light of the bow lantern. "Maybe you think you're a big Swede, too," he said.

Tad didn't say anything. He just stood holding on to the horses' heads looking back at Lupes. In a minute Lupes asked, "If you got any other ideas you can tell me now."

But Tad didn't say anything and after another minute Lupes started off up the driveway. He gave Tad his elbow into the ribs as he went by, and Tad took it. It was a good trick of Lupes's, using the elbow like that. He'd won more than one fight using it. Tad felt the pain go into his side and hang there, but he didn't move. He didn't even look up when Casper came along the deck and looked down.

Casper said, "*He* feels pretty good."

"He thinks he's God Almighty riding the universe," Tad said.

"You better not rile him," Casper said.

"Run out the bridge, will you?" Tad said.

"My Jesus, Tad. What you aiming to do?"

"I said run out the bridge."

"You putting the horses on?"

"What do you think I'm doing?"

"I won't be a party to it," Casper said.

"Oh, God, Casper. I won't tell on you."

"You'll swear that, Bible oath?"

"All right. I've swore," Tad said. Casper ran the bridge out. He was shivering as bad as the horses. The water was running off the end of his nose. He said, "I'm going on up to the Rose Tavern. I don't know where the horses are, see?"

"You can go to hell," Tad said.

Casper said, "You hadn't ought to tell me that, Tad." He sounded hurt. "I only got two bits pocket money," he said. He went off after Lupes.

Tad put the horses on board and left them in the stable. Then he reached back of the manger he slept in and got his dry shirt and took it down to the cabin and changed by the stove. He didn't often get a chance to do that. For a while he considered hunting for Lupes's money box, but he thought it would take too much time. He was getting into a cold anger. The place where Lupes had elbowed him showed a bruise already and it ached. He thought he would like to kill Lupes, but he thought it was more likely Lupes would kill him. He didn't care. He was chilled all through from the rain and he wanted to get up to Rose Tavern himself and get something to drink. Mrs. Andrews would surely give him something.

Mrs. Andrews greeted him at the kitchen door. She was a middle-aged woman with a stout pink face and she wore a boatman's cap on her hair. "My God, Tad Brock," she said. "What you doing here?"

"Hello, Mrs. Andrews," Tad said. "Is Lupes in the bar?"

"Yes. He's telling everybody how he licked Johnson. Is that fact?"

"He licked him proper," Tad said.

"That's what he says. He told me he'd left you minding the horses. You better not let him see you. I won't tell though. Give us a kiss, Tad. My, you've growed. You're pretty near a grown man, I'd say." She laughed. "Someday you'll be having your own boat and then you'll come to Mabel's, won't you?" She giggled at him. Tad grinned back. Ever since he'd first come that had been a joke between them, whether he'd grow up fast enough to be a man before she lost her looks.

He said bitterly, "I won't get away from him for four years yet, though."

"You look cold, Tad. Here, I'll fetch in some rum and lemon and you can put some water from the kettle in it."

"I've got no money."

She laughed.

"You can buy me a brooch with colored stones when you bring your boat, Tad." She gave her petticoat a twist when she turned and he could see her legs. For a stout woman she had thin legs. She moved light and quick on them. Tad shivered a little. She must have been something in her time.

When she came back, he asked her where she had come from.

"You been asking me that before," she said. "I came here to get in the country. The doctor told me to." She looked around. "I've not done bad, either. But it's not like New York."

"New York City?" he asked.

"Where do you think, silly?"

"I never been there."

"That's the place to go. These towns up here, they call them cities. But they haven't got anything. Tad, boy, you ought to see New York. Museums and menageries and theaters. Fine carriages on the streets and fine ladies in them and gentlemen in London-made pants. You see men in Syracuse and Utica that think they're wearing fine clothes." She laughed scornfully. "Here's your rum," she said. "You better drink it quick, and get back to the *Belle*. Lupes told me you was walking the horses on the towpath and he feels pretty big right now."

"Lupes can go to hell," Tad said.

He was thinking about New York City and the fine things money could do. They said America was the place where anybody could get to be President, or a rich man, but it seemed to him you had to have money to start with. Five dollars wouldn't keep him from getting sent back to Lupes. He said something about it to Mrs. Andrews and it annoyed her.

"Why, Tad Brock. I've told you the same thing myself. It's true. In four years you'll be your own man and you can do anything."

"I can't wait four years," he said.

"Why don't you run away, then?" she asked suddenly.

"I'm bound out to Lupes. He'd send the sheriff after me."

"To New York?" She laughed.

"He could put a piece in the papers."

"My God, Tad," she said. "Do you think people in New York read papers from up here — like the *Gospel Messenger,* or the *Troy Watchman,* or even the *Argus* in Albany?"

"Is that so?"

"Yes, it is. Besides, once you get a job and make some money and buy some decent clothes nobody'd ever know you. You get a haircut by a good barber and you'd look like a gentleman, Tad."

She went out again and Tad sat with the hot rum in his hand and watched the rain tracking down the windowpanes. He thought it would be easy to slip out back now and walk cross country to the Syracuse road and find a wagon heading east. But it would be easier if he could find some of Lupes's money. He had right enough to it — he'd never had a cent, where other drivers had been hired on for eleven dollars a month though they hadn't always got it.

He finished the rum, and one of Mrs. Andrews's hired girls came in and smiled at him.

"Where you going?"

He said cautiously, "I've got to get back to the boat."

"Well, wait a minute. You better have something to eat with that drink."

She got a couple of doughnuts from a jar and gave them to him, and stood watching him with a smile.

She was a nice girl, sort of foolish looking, and she worked in the kitchen. Her father had an understanding with Mrs. Andrews that she wasn't to work up front. Mrs. Andrews was faithful to the contract, but in the summer season the girl sometimes had to work in the bar.

She said now, "Lupes McCagg was just asking if you had the team out by the boat and he wanted me to look out the front door. But I knew where you was. I had to laugh at him. I said you was in here. You better go into the bar. He wants you in there."

Tad looked at her.

"You told him I was in here?"

"Yes. He's acting kind of mad." She giggled. Tad looked at her bitterly. Then he realized that she wasn't to blame. She wasn't right in the head. He felt all his anger come together slowly. He said, "You can tell Lupes I'm at the boat. If he wants to find me, he can come out in the wet."

He knew he was a fool as soon as the rain hit his face. He might just as well clear out, now, while he had time. If he was caught he wouldn't get anything worse then than Lupes would do to him now. But he kept on walking down to the canal.

A boat had come in from the west and another boat was down the bend heading towards them. Its steersman gave a toot on his horn and the sound was weak in the rain. The lights came slowly up to the light on the *Western Belle* and the whole towpath showed up bright: the water, the teams dragging in, the driver boys slogging along in the mud, and the wet budded branches of the nearest trees.

Lupes McCagg came down the driveway from Rose Tavern with his shadow thrown back from his heels, and Casper, walking just behind him, was saying, "Honest to God, he's a crazy boy. I didn't know nothing about it, Lupes. He must have put the bridge out himself. Honest to God, Lupes."

Lupes didn't pay any attention to him. He walked under the noses of the westbound team and came up to Tad and said, "Where's the horses?"

"On the boat."

Tad felt himself getting small in his inside. But he let the coils of his whip slip off his wrist and he flicked them back out straight.

"I told you to stay here. Where was you?"

"In Rose Tavern," Tad said. He didn't have much voice. What there was of it didn't sound like his. He yelled all of a sudden, "You keep your hands off me, Lupes."

"Getting kind of scared, ain't you?" Lupes asked. "You drop that whip."

Lupes was showing a little of his liquor. He wasn't unsteady on his feet, but his eyes shifted up and down as if he didn't see bright with them all the time. His face was flushed and he kept drawing his breath slowly. All the time he shuffled his feet a little to edge in on Tad.

The other boats had stopped and the steersmen had come up onto the bows to see what was happening. A cook off one of the boats hollered, "What's stopping us, Clem?"

The man said, "It's Lupes McCagg. He's going to lick his driver."

Casper edged up to the speaker and informed him of the fight with Swede Johnson.

"Honest to God," he said. "It was a fight."

"The boy's crazy. I had a crazy driver once. I had to get rid of him."

Tad saw Lupes make a move. He swung the whip. But his hand wasn't right and Lupes caught the lash on his arm. He gave a yank and pulled Tad off balance, ripping the whip out of his hand.

"Now, by God," he said.

Tad felt himself kicked back into the mud and lay there getting his breath. He heard the whip hiss but the lash overreached and bit mud on his far side, losing most of the force of the blow. Tad scrambled up before Lupes could swing back. It was sheer luck, catching Lupes with his right hand drawn back and anchored by the whip. Tad hit at the open face with all his might.

In all the fights Tad had seen, he had only once seen Lupes McCagg knocked off his feet. It shocked him to see how easily it had happened now. The thick short body swung from the knuckles of his fist and spun sidewise. Lupes's arms went up, letting go the whip, and he went headfirst into the canal.

Tad picked up the whip. Nobody else said a word, not even Casper who stood openmouthed, with the water from his nose striking on his chin. They all listened to Lupes floundering in the water and then they saw him lay hold of the grass and mud to haul himself out. There was a strange look of confusion on his face. Then Casper shouted suddenly, "My God, Tad, don't do it!"

But Tad was set. He could not have stopped himself if he wanted to. The whip cracked like a pistol and the lash hit Lupes's cheek and laid it open from ear to chin.

Lupes's cry was swallowed by the canal. All the boaters came running up to the spot, suddenly shouting for a rope or a boat hook, and one of the steersmen laid his hands on Tad's shoulder.

The man shouted for help. But Tad threw him off and jumped back. "Let go of me," he yelled.

"He's crazy. Look out for him."

Casper said, "My God, it was murder."

The cook had come out under a broken umbrella.

"Look out," she shrieked. "He's getting away."

Two of the men turned.

"He went over that knoll." She pointed wildly with the broken umbrella. "See, he's just climbing the fence."

One of the steersmen said, "He ain't my driver."

"I wouldn't go after him if he was."

The man with the boat hook said, "I got Lupes."

They pulled Lupes McCagg up onto the towpath.

Everybody looked down at him. "He ain't dead," said Casper after a moment. "But he'll have to be drained."

CHARLIE PHISTER'S FAMOUS BEE SHOT

❖❖❖❖❖❖❖❖❖❖❖❖❖❖❖❖❖❖❖❖❖❖❖❖❖❖❖❖❖❖❖❖❖

Not many people get to be famous. Most never do. Some may become talked about for a time, and you could say the same of frogs or man-eating tigers or high butterfat cows. They make their mark and that's about all of it for them. But once in a great while it happens to someone to become famous a second time around, which was how it was for Charlie Phister, at the tag end of his life, when he turned seventy-four years old.

I

It was just making daybreak when he woke up. He could hear the roosters in Jed Proctor's chicken yard a quarter mile down the canal rousting the phlegm from their throats to make ready for crowing. It sounded as if the young roosters had a harder time doing it than the older birds, which was queer — it being just the opposite in humans. But if it came to that, two legs was about the only thing men and roosters had in common, unless you counted crowing. Not that Charlie felt much like crowing that morning. At least not after he'd looked at the calendar behind the stove and seen what the date was. October 19. Sunday. October 19 had been Sunday, too, back in 1828 when he'd got born. It was 1902 now, which made him seventy-four years old. That didn't puff his brisket any. Every year added on to his life now meant one less year yet to come.

When he was a little child his mother used to tell him getting borned on Sunday was a lucky thing. Such people, she said, got blessed in life. She was three parts Tuscarora Indian but a strong practicing Christian. Little Charlie believed her, but nothing special ever happened to him to prove it. After she died he moved into Boonville village and made enough money doing chores for people to pay his board at Mrs. Brennan's boardinghouse. People said he didn't have a lot upstairs but considered him harmless. He just got along. So it came as a surprise when in 1861 at the commencement of the Civil War, he volunteered in the Ninety-seventh New York Infantry.

The regiment did its training right in Boonville and when it went off to war on March 12, 1862, into a howling blizzard, on a train of sixteen coach cars with Old Butterfly and a helper engine on the head end, nobody thought to see Charlie again, if in fact anybody put any mind on him at all.

But Charlie sure enough came back. He had gone through every battle the regiment was in, which was about the whole list for the Army of the Potomac — from Cedar Mountain to Hatcher's Run, but there he lost four fingers when he was reaching up to wipe sweat off his left ear. A cannonball did the job as neat as a giant pair of pinking shears. Anyone without Charlie's luck, it was said, would have lost not only his fingers but his whole hand, his ear, and his head as well. So he didn't get to Appomattox for Lee's surrender. But he did manage to rejoin the Ninety-seventh when it was mustered out in Washington, D.C., the middle of July

'65, and he came back with the rest of the boys who'd made it on the railroad cars to Boonville.

Once back in Boonville he would sit evenings in the parlor of Mrs. Brennan's boardinghouse and tell anybody willing to listen how it had been in this battle or that one. To hear the way he told it, though he gave considerable credit to General Ulysses Grant also, Charlie Phister played a mighty important part in every one of those battles. There were plenty in the Union Army, he maintained, that knew him not just as Private Phister but as Sure-Shot Charlie.

Most people took these stories as so much bunkum, the kind of stories Charlie used to tell before he went to war about catching a six-pound speckled trout out of Horn Lake or shooting a four-hundred-and-fifty-pound buck deer.

Only Dianthea Atwell thought different. She worked as hired girl in Mrs. Brennan's house, being her niece, and she took care of bedrooms as well as waiting table and washing dishes. She found a box in Charlie's top dresser drawer with his war souvenirs in it, and when she looked inside what she saw convinced her Charlie was no bunkum-talker but the real McCoy. Besides the Civil War Medal almost every veteran sported, there was a Merit Medal in that box. At first she just admired what she saw but after a while her feelings sharpened into something else. Nobody else she knew or had even heard of had a Merit Medal on top of being a top-notch sharpshooter and being in all those battles as well. She was thirty-five years old and, though a neat-enough person to look at, she wasn't gaining any in the beauty race. So she not only fell in love with Charlie, she married him.

That wasn't so surprising. All Atwells were strong-minded folks and when she saw a chance to catch herself a husband she wouldn't have let him go for Hallelujah. Besides, Charlie wasn't a man who could say no easy, except to turn down a job that called for hard work. Still, it isn't certain he said yes to Dianthea. He just went along with her to the Presbyterian minister's house; they went inside; and when they came out they were Mr. and Mrs. Phister.

Getting married was a very good thing for Charlie Phister. Dianthea looked out for him and made him comfortable. She knew he wasn't fitted to make any big cut in the world. He'd never make them rich. So she found the kind of work that would suit him, being as little like real work as possible. She got him a job tending lock on the Black River Canal. Being a war veteran entitled him to preference, she discovered, and she didn't leave off pestering the district superintendent and even the State Engineer's Office until she not only got the job for him but the very lock she had her eye on, Number 70, a bit more than a fat mile below Boonville village. It had what she considered was the nicest lock-tender's shanty on the whole canal. Partly she liked it because it was bigger than most. It had a narrow bedroom alongside the kitchen, which was good sized as well. And then it had a pump from a good well right in the kitchen so a woman didn't have to go out and carry in her water.

She kept the lock, too, just about as much as he did, for Charlie was a deep sleeper. So, when a boat horn sounded early in the morning, it was most liable to be Dianthea who was out to meet it with the lock all trimmed and ready. She could manage the job every bit as good as Charlie and he didn't mind her doing it. The only thing he wouldn't let her do was to operate the gate of the waste weir, which controlled the depth of water in the summit level above Lock 70, all the way back to Boonville.

There was a marker on the far side of the canal marked off in feet and inches and it was the lock-tender's job to keep the water level right about four feet. If it started going up, you had to raise the waste gate, but you couldn't raise it too much or the level at the top end of the summit level would start dropping.

First thing every morning Charlie would come out of the shanty and walk the hundred feet or so up the towpath to where it crossed the waste weir on a bridge, studying the flow of the canal as he went. When he got to the bridge he would give the crank that raised the gate a nudge or two, look over his shoulder again to the marker on the far side, and then operate the crank till the gate either had shut down to what seemed right or had raised till a strong flow of water rushed out on the weir. He would lean his forearms on the cross member of the waste-gate frame and just stand there, watching the water race under his feet and down over the big rock slide that dumped it into Sink Hole Pond. Nobody knew for certain how the water ran out of the pond. There must have been an opening somewhere in the bottom, and once it got underground in that limestone country, water could go anywhere it was a-mind to.

Leaning on the cross member, his eyes looking beyond the smooth roll of the water where it started over the falls, Charlie Phister would feel a stillness stealing into him. Times were when he seemed to hear the water threading the underground wrinkles of the earth.

Seeing him from her kitchen door as he leaned there lost in the entrancement of his mind, Dianthea's face would crinkle up with fondness. It was the Indian in him, she thought, working at his personal medicine. Nobody she had ever known could foretell the weather like her Charlie or find woods berries in a drought year or lift a log to show her a nest of black salamanders spotted over with yellow spots like small gold currencies. Living with Charlie wasn't the same as living with other men. Oh, he might look brown and squat-built as a bear carved out of a hickory butt, but for her he was the best. She would hesitate before calling him in to breakfast. She knew he would come all right, even though he might take a time to turn her way. He'd told her, once, that she cooked real good. The only thing he ever found fault with her for was dying, which she did, suddenly, in spring sixteen years after they got married.

II

A few people wondered how Charlie would get along without Dianthea looking after him, but they didn't trouble their minds about him very long. As far as boatmen locking through Number 70 could tell he didn't show much difference except it would be him instead of her that came out to trim the lock for an early-morning boat. His clothes got to look a bit more worn as time passed, but they seemed pretty clean. He planted a bunch of bachelor's buttons by the shanty's front step the way she'd done and he sat on the stoop in his straight kitchen chair. It all looked just the same except for her empty rocker.

Inside the shanty it was like that, too. Sometimes a woman off a boat would find a reason to look inside, the way a woman does, but she found the kitchen picked up and pretty near as proud as Dianthea used to keep it, but crowded-like. Charlie had built a bunk bed for himself in the corner of it. He didn't sleep any more in the extra room Dianthea'd laid such store by and he didn't seem to like it when a visiting woman made as if to look inside. All the living he had to do he did right in the kitchen, or tending the lock outside. The farthest he went was up the towpath to the waste weir or down to Proctor's to buy eggs and butter, or once in a while a chicken. Any grocery trading he needed he got done for him by a boatman or his woman hauling by.

Some talked as if he had become a hermit. But that wasn't so. Hermits took off into the woods and lived entirely by themselves in shacks no better than lean-tos with the front closed in. They talked only with toads and snakes, or occasionally a skunk if he happened to come calling. When they did come out of the woods, maybe once or twice in a year, it was as hard to understand the words they used as it was a man talking with a cleft palate and a wad of spruce gum.

Charlie wasn't that way at all even if he did keep to himself most of the time. He liked it whenever a party rowed down from Boonville for a Sunday picnic at the falls into Sink Hole Pond. He would even open the waste gate, if the falls were low, to send a gush of water onto them, and if some city cousin from Schenectady or Syracuse happened to be showing off on them rocks at the time and got a sousing, that didn't hurt nothing either.

Once in a while he would get asked to join the party, but he didn't feel easy with all the commotion and would sit off to one side and only speak when somebody asked him something. To make himself feel easier he would pick up a piece of wood and whittle shavings off it. One day one of the children, who didn't feel no better in a loud party than Charlie did himself, asked him what he was whittling.

"Nothing," Charlie told her. "Just making shavings."

"Why don't you whittle something for me?" she asked.

He turned his square brown face towards her but didn't answer for so long she began to get scared of him. Just in time to stop her from running off, he asked her, "Why do you think I'd whittle something for you?"

"Well," she said, "it would be better than making just shavings. Who wants them?"

Still staring at her he considered that for a minute. Then he asked what she wanted him to carve.

"Oh, an animal. A cat, maybe. Or a frog."

"All right," Charlie said. "I'll try a frog."

And he did, while she edged up closer to watch him. It ended up a recognizable frog and she ran back

shouting to the picnic. Which was how Charlie got
started into carving little creatures for keepsakes. Even
when there were no picnickers around he would try his
hand at some new animal, and one day Jervis Hanna
coming up in his boat, the *Effie & May,* said Charlie
ought to sell some of them carvings and offered to take
a sampling up to Ano's Notion Store. Rudy Ano
thought they might sell and agreed to take a dozen,
charging fifty cents apiece for them and sending back
twenty-five to Charlie. So Charlie got money enough
out of his whittling to keep him in sugar most of the
time and it helped to keep his mind off Dianthea in
slack times of the boating season. He would keep col-
lecting pieces of wood that looked easy to carve and
now and then a boatman would slip a short piece of
scantling off a load of lumber. Every morning, too, he
would get out his old waterstone and spend a half hour
whetting up his jackknife.

And that was the first thing he did on Sunday, the
nineteenth of October, 1902, on his seventy-fourth
birthday, after pulling on his pants and tying the laces
in his shoes. He dipped the flat red stone into a pail of
water and began whetting the big blade first. He took
his time, making circles with the edge of the blade
against the stone. Then he turned the blade over and
made more circles back. He spent four or five minutes
at it. When he got it to where it seemed to him it must
be getting sharp, he tried it on the back of his wrist.
Like many people with Indian blood he didn't have
any body hair to speak of, but there were a few grown
out since the last time he'd tried the blade, and they
shaved off at a touch. He put the knife back in the pail

of water and pulled it out and shook it dry. Then he went at the little blade, giving extra attention to the point of it. When he got it to the edge he wanted, he folded up the blade and put the knife in his pocket.

After that he threw a couple of extra chunks in his cookstove, pumped some water in the kettle, which he put on to boil, buttoned the three bottom buttons of his shirt, hauled his hat off the door peg and put it on the back of his head, and went out on the stoop. It was a cold morning and mist was rising off the canal, even out of the deep coffin of the lock. The sweet-sour smell of fermenting grasses filled the air, and Charlie, who liked it, sucked it down into his chest as he turned up the towpath to check the waste weir.

The marker showed the level three inches high so he turned to the waste gate to raise it a notch or two. That was when his eyes first lit on the bumblebee. It was sitting on the cross member, and just as Charlie spotted it the sun broke through the trees on the east rim of the valley and sent its first beams down directly on the waste gate, Charlie, and the bee.

It was a very large bumblebee. Charlie couldn't recollect ever having seen a bigger bee and he approached it in kind of a precautious way. But the bee paid him no mind. It rested on the cross member as if it had just lighted there. Something about it didn't look quite right to Charlie. The white coat of frost had begun to melt away from its feet. Still, it was a handsome bee, about as handsome in its plushy black and yellow striping as any bee could hope to look.

Charlie was deliberate in the way he came near to it. A bee as big as this one was bound to have a considerable stinger. He wasn't a man to monkey with any bee unnecessarily. But gradually he put his head down till he could examine it real close up, from maybe ten inches away, and he went over it almost hair by hair and one foot after another. He saw how the bee's feelers reached forward from the back of its head and the way its stinger stuck out from its back end. And still the consarned insect didn't move. So Charlie came to the conclusion that it was sick, or if it wasn't sick it must be dead, very likely froze to death. He moved his lips a little, Charlie that is, not the bee, and he reached out a forefinger to touch it. But at the last instant he drew it back, feeling still precautious. And then he got his knife out of his pocket, opening the long blade, still moving slow and careful, and finally he touched the bee's back end with the point of the blade.

It didn't take off, but it moved a trifle on legs as stiff as wires and Charlie saw that for a fact he had a dead bumblebee on the cross member of his waste gate. Well, sir, that was a relieving thing to have found out and Charlie made as if to close up his knife. But then a notion took him. He never did make out whether it came from inside his head or maybe from someplace outside of it. But all of a sudden he saw that here was a way to find out how really sharp he'd got his knife.

No question of holding the insect with one hand. It had to be a free cut. Slow and careful, again, he put the edge of the blade back of the head, against whatever it was joined a bee's head to its body, and drew the blade slowly and gently towards himself. And sure enough, the blade sliced down and through the neck, the head dropped off without the body even falling over. Charlie stared down at the two parts admiring what his knife had done. No person could deny that it was sharp.

He closed the blade, then cranked the waste gate up and leaned against the cross member to watch the water frothing under him on its way to the falls into Sink Hole Pond. After a minute his eye wandered back to the body of the bumblebee next to his hand with the head lying just ahead of it, and without putting it to any kind of thought he snapped his finger off his thumb to shoot the head out over the racing water. He couldn't see it hit the water but in his mind's eye he could follow it over the falls and down into the pond. He wondered how far it might go from there. He had a moment's notion to send the body after the head, but the body looked so handsome there in the sunlight that he left it be. After all, not every man was lucky enough to take the head off a bee as big as that.

Feeling real satisfied he turned back down the towpath to his shanty to get himself a breakfast.

III

Being his birthday and Sunday combined, Charlie considered he was maybe entitled to one a little special. He started by mixing up a batter of buckwheat flour and buttermilk, which last Mrs. Proctor had sent up the day before as a free gift. When he had the batter ready, he fried himself some bacon. Then he went to the cupboard for a jug of maple syrup that had come as part pay last April for sugaring in Proctor's bush. With those items in hand he poured his batter into the fry pan and made himself a stack of buckwheat cakes. It made a pretty good breakfast even for a man as solid-built as Charlie, especially washing it down with tea from the kettle he always kept simmering on the back of the stove. There were plenty of people couldn't take down a cup of Charlie's tea and stay setting on their chairs; it was strong enough, Joe Dempster said, to make a porcupine shed his quills. Charlie, though, thought nothing of taking three or four cups in a row.

By the time he got finished eating and had cleaned up, the sun had climbed over the valley rim and, there not being any wind, the day had turned so warm and nice he went outdoors onto the porch with his knife and a piece of white pine wood and sat down to whittle out a turtledove. His thoughts wandered some over the seventy-four years of his life. He remembered his ma telling it was lucky for a person to get borned on Sunday, and he guessed it was true since he had got through the Civil War only losing the fingers off his left hand where so many more of the old Ninety-seventh regiment had never made it back to Boonville. And he had been lucky for a fact in marrying Dianthea. He recollected how much she was pleased when they moved into the shanty here at Lock 70, especially when she saw the wallpaper with its scenes of Egypt. Oh, she said the pyramids were fine, the sphynx too, and the palm trees, and the temples with broken pillars, but what she liked the best was the picture, wherever it showed up in the pattern, of those Egypt women around a well with great water jars on their heads which they would have to carry all the way back to their homes. Dianthea would take hold of the pump handle beside the sink and fill her kettle and smile a secret kind of smile. Charlie always liked to watch her doing that.

But when it came to what his old ma had said about a Sunday-born person being blessed, he didn't feel too sure. The way things had turned out he liked thinking about the back parts of his life more than whatever it was that was to come. So this birthday morning he put his mind on the good years gone by, and as he thought, his knife commenced to whittle slower. The sunshine got warmer and warmer on his shoulders; and the running sound of water tumbling down the sluice went on and on, and after a while he dozed off. He was that way when Brad Considine with two of his pals came up the towpath from Proctor's farm.

Ordinarily the three of them when they were out on the loose made a considerable ruckus, hooting and yelling and horsing around in general; but this morning instead of turning up to kid old Charlie and generally make fun of him, they had come to get his serious opinion. Brad, whose father was Philo Considine, feed and coal merchant as well as half owner of Purdy's Lumber Mill and by a long chalk the richest man in Boonville, had inherited from his young uncle Ted Moody what was practically a brand new Winchester .22 caliber rifle. It had an octagonal barrel with a magazine underneath that would hold sixteen cartridges.

Now, when you are fourteen or fifteen years old it kind of sobers you down to have something left to you in a man's will, and when that man is your favorite uncle and still pretty young himself and dead from being smothered in the biggest slide in fifteen years in the Paragon Plaster Company's sand and gravel pit it is likely to sober you down even more. It made Brad Considine mighty choosy who he would let touch the rifle, still less shoot it off. Only his very best friends, Alvah Corey and Freeman Jones, were allowed to do that.

They had taken it out the week before to hunt frogs in Murdock's fish pond. They had seen plenty of frogs, but they hadn't hit a one and it got so upsetting for the bunch of them that they had to chase up an excuse. Brad said he thought the frogs were too wild to hold still for the bullet to hit them, but Alvah had to point out that Brad had shot three times at the same frog without its moving from its place. Freeman said he thought maybe the rifle was mis-sighted or possibly didn't even shoot straight; but Brad wouldn't hear a word about the barrel being out of true. They were pretty worked up by the time they had used up all their cartridges, and they put the question to Philo, Brad's pa, when they got home.

Philo Considine said that Uncle Ted had put a deal of store in that gun and doubted if there was much could be wrong with it. He himself was no hand with a rifle, never had been nor never wanted to be, so he couldn't really judge. But he suggested they go and show it to Charlie Phister. Charlie, he pointed out, might not amount to much but he had been a sharp-shooter in the old Ninety-seventh volunteers that some people also called the Conklin Rifles. A sharpshooter in a hot contest like the Civil War had to shoot pretty straight, in fact straighter than the man against him, if he wanted to go on living. Charlie had come back alive. Stood to reason then, he told the boys, that Charlie would be able to judge the worth of a rifle better than most. He had business to do with Proctor the next Sunday and would drive them down to the farm so they could come home along the towpath, stopping to show the gun to Charlie Phister on their way. Which was what they did.

They could tell from a quite a way off that Charlie was having a nod in the sun, but they didn't give him the kind of old whammeroo they would have other times. Even setting in his kitchen chair on that dinky little stoop, he looked bigger and heavier than they seemed to remember him, and it was a minute before Brad got his nerve up to say, "Mr. Phister."

Charlie didn't move. They could see he was still off in the land of nod. Freeman Jones whispered, "You ain't ever called him 'Mr. Phister' before, Brad. Maybe he don't know it's his own name." Freeman was the youngest of the three and ordinarily the other two didn't think much of his opinion. But Brad had to admit he was right this time, so he said, "Hey, Charlie!" a good deal louder than he'd said, "Mr. Phister."

But Charlie showed no change and Alvah Corey suddenly got kind of white around the gills. "You don't suppose he's dead, do you?"

Brad looked close. "No," he said. "I can see his chest move under his shirt."

He reached out and touched Charlie on the side of the neck. It was an amazing thing, the way Charlie came to. His head raised slowly. Then his hands lifted just as slow out of his lap and the one with the knife came over to meet the left hand holding the unfinished turtledove between thumb and brown fingerless palm, his eyes came open and the knife sliced a tiny shaving off the back of the dove's neck. Not till then did he take in the three boys standing around him with Brad in front, holding the rifle.

He showed no surprise. His eyes dropped to his hands and he used the knife again. "You boys want to see me about something?" he asked.

"Yes, sir, Mr. Phister," Brad said. "We'd like to know what you think of this gun."

Charlie's eyes raised until they had the Winchester in view.

"Looks nice," he said. "What's wrong with it?"

"I don't know. I got it from my uncle Ted. He left it to me in his will," Brad said. "We took it out frog hunting last week, but we didn't hit no frogs at all."

"I ain't surprised," Charlie said. "Whooping and hollering all the while."

"We didn't holler," Freeman protested. "We didn't make no noise hardly at all."

"You ought to seen where the bullets went," Charlie observed. "Shooting into the water for frogs."

"We did, Charlie," Brad said. "We saw the bullets go in the water, only they didn't none of them go into a frog."

"Then you wasn't shooting straight, I guess."

"I shot frogs before," Alvah told him. "Only not with this here rifle."

"Well, what you want me to do?" Charlie asked.

"We thought maybe you could take a shot or two with it," Brad said. "And see how it shoots for you."

Charlie hoisted himself off his chair and went into the kitchen to leave the unfinished turtledove on the table. He had a drink of water from the dipper in the bucket under the pump to clear his head after sleeping the way he had. He came out again on the stoop and told Brad to let him have the rifle.

"Loaded?" Charlie asked.

"Yes," Brad said, "but there ain't a cartridge in the breech."

"Pump action," Charlie said, mostly to himself. "Never owned no pump-action gun."

He balanced the .22 on his fingerless left hand.

"Pretty little gun," he muttered, as if he was talking to himself. "Not much heft to it. But it's a pretty little gun, all right."

Brad looked pleased. He nodded.

"I brought along a piece of paper for a target. Where do you want me to fasten it up, Charlie?"

"Nowheres," Charlie told him. "Ain't going in for target shooting. One shot will tell what this little gun can do."

"You got to shoot at something," Alvah Corey said. "You got to have a mark of some kind to tell where the bullet hits."

"Sure," Charlie said. "But I don't need no paper. Now look there," he went on, suddenly. "Durned if there ain't a bumblebee up there on top of the waste gate. You see it, you fellers?"

They turned to stare at the waste gate, maybe a hundred feet up the towpath. Sure enough, there, on the cross member, was a bumblebee. It looked awful small that far away and Freeman Jones said, "You ain't aiming to hit it from here, are you, Mr. Phister?"

"I wouldn't likely hit it without aiming, would I?" Charlie asked.

He raised the stock to his shoulder and sighted on the bee, but then he lowered the gun and looked at the three boys.

"If I shot at that big bumblebee," he said, "and blowed it all to bits we wouldn't know if this here rifle is really any good. So what I'll do is shoot that durned bee's head off. If I do that you'll know this gun is all right."

Once more he raised the gun to his shoulder, sighted with great care while the boys held their breath, and very deliberately pulled the trigger.

At the snap of the rifle Charlie cradled it in his left arm and patted the breech.

"This here's a good gun," he said with gravity. "Real good. You're in luck, Brad."

They stared at him, then looked back at the waste gate. The bumblebee was still on the cross timber.

"I didn't see the bullet strike nowhere," Alvah said in a voice dripping with disbelief.

"Me neither," Brad said.

"No," Charlie said. "That bee's head is maybe three-quarter inch above the timber. The bullet wouldn't hit the timber if it knocked the head off of him."

Freeman Jones took off for the waste gate. As he came up to it he stopped short and stared. Then he started yelling, "Come here and look! Charlie's shot the head right off him!"

The other two rushed up the towpath to join him.

"That's right," Brad shouted back at Charlie. "You shot his head off, all right, Mr. Phister."

His voice was awestruck. So was Alvah Corey's. "I bet there ain't anybody in the whole of New York State made a shot like that, Mr. Phister."

"Ain't nobody done a shot this good in the whole U.S.A.," Freeman Jones said. "Nobody in the entire universe, I bet," he corrected himself, his voice sliding up in a sort of uncreased falsetto. The other two nodded.

Alvah Corey picked up the bee's body with great care and carried it down to the shanty.

"We got to take this back to town," he said. "We got to show it to people so they'll know. You got a box or something we could put it in? I wouldn't want to hold it in my hand all the whole way," he said. "In case I fell down or something."

Charlie looked down at the bee's body.

"Yep," he said. "Cleaner shot than I thought."

He handed the .22 back to Brad and went into his shanty, where he rummaged till he found an old tin box and some rags, in which the boys carefully packed the body. Then they said good-bye and started home along the towpath with no idea any more of hunting frogs.

Charlie went into his shanty. When he came out he had the unfinished turtledove in his hand. Sitting down again, he got his knife out of his pocket. A kind of smile bent his lips as he went back to carving, but he wasn't thinking of past times any more.

IV

Well, sir, when the boys had told Brad's pa about the shot and showed Mr. Considine the bumblebee in evidence, he took the matter up in a big way. He called up Willard Harvey, the editor of the *Boonville Her-*

ald, and when Mr. Harvey heard the story and saw the body of the bumblebee, he said he wanted the boys to come to the office with him and each one to swear out an affidavit, which started Freeman Jones crying until Brad and Alvah told him scornfully that it wouldn't hurt him none. After which Mr. Harvey said he had to have pictures taken. He wanted the three boys' picture and he wanted Charlie Phister's. He wanted the picture taken down at Charlie's shanty by Lock 70. So he hired a rig from Joe Hemphill's livery stable and when Joe heard what it was all about he drove them himself, stopping on the way down Main Street to pick up George Turpin, the photographer.

When they reached the shanty, Charlie was still whittling at his turtledove and he grumbled some about having his afternoon disturbed. But Mr. Harvey told him he was a famous man now and had to show consideration for the public, who had a right to know. Of course, Charlie couldn't stand against that so he left off his whittling and got off his chair and asked where did they want him to stand. Mr. Harvey didn't have any real idea but said something about maybe it ought to be with the three boys, maybe with his arms across the shoulders of the two tallest ones with Freeman Jones in front holding the rifle.

Brad wouldn't hear of that. If anybody was going to hold his rifle in a picture it was going to be himself. But when George Turpin suggested that the three boys go to stand at the waste gate and point to where the bee had been while Charlie Phister aimed the gun as if he was going to shoot it, Brad agreed. So it was taken that way, and then because the boys would look

kind of small in the picture, George took another picture of them on the stoop of Charlie's shanty, with
Charlie standing back of them. Brad was holding his
gun in this one, though.

The story made a handsome spread in the *Herald.*
There were the two photographs, and in between them
a picture, taken real close, of the bumblebee. Anybody
could see it had no head. The story with the pictures
told how it had happened Charles Phister had been
asked to show his skill. And that wasn't so surprising
considering Mr. Phister's record as a sharpshooter in
the Civil War. After the story came out in the *Herald,*
the newspapers in Utica and Rome and Syracuse carried it in their own versions and the *New York
Tribune* sent a reporter up from New York City.

Charlie Phister had become a famous man. People
in Boonville began to think about him in a different
way from what they had. He was asked now to head the
Memorial Day parade to the cemetery every spring and
when the Fourth of July came around Charlie led the
marching notables, right behind the band, up Main
and Schuyler streets to the Fairgrounds. Anybody visiting Boonville was told who Charlie Phister was.

When it came time for Charlie to die, Boonville
gave him a finer burial than any other citizen in its
entire history. The procession to the cemetery
stretched all the way from Brendan Griffis's funeral
parlor to the railroad crossing on South Main Street. It
was headed by the Boonville band but there were sev-
eral other bands including the fife and drum band
from Camden in their colonial uniforms. There were

stories in the newspapers headed CELEBRATED VETERAN DIES and FIRED FAMOUS SHOT. People all over kept saying how Charlie Phister had put Boonville on the map. But between you and me it isn't likely that old Charlie cared a hoot.

THE NIGHT RAIDER

❖❖❖

THE FARM BUILDINGS stood in the river valley, with a rushing brook separating them from the big house in which we lived. My father liked to feel that someday the farm might pay for itself, and he had the idea that the bigger it was, the more likely it was to do so. He kept adding to the dairy herd until there were almost eighty head of milking cows. With old Woodlawn, the Holstein bull, and the calves and young stock the herd numbered one hundred. There were two farm teams and an odd horse to rake hay and pull the potato hiller and take the three great milk cans to the cheese factory.

In the carriage barn he kept three more horses. He had a hen house full of Rhode Island Reds and Plymouth Rocks, a hog house with Black Berkshire pigs, sheep that pastured on the uplands in summer, a flock of turkeys that also ranged on the uplands every day, Indian Runner ducks in the brook, and finally he acquired a flock of guinea hens. It was because of them that the raider was drawn to the farm.

I was seven then, and for me life began each morning only when I had crossed the brook to the farm buildings. I would stop first at the farmhouse where the superintendent, old Nelson, lived with his wife, Mrs. Goodwell, to find out what would be going on that day. Life on a big farm is a very complex operation, but Nelson had it all at his fingertips.

He was a tall, heavy-built, quiet-spoken man with shoulders so rounded that he seemed almost hunch-backed. As he explained it, his shoulders got that way during the Battle of Gettysburg. He had been fourteen then, a slim, long-boned boy, who had volunteered to bring in wounded soldiers. According to Mrs. Good-well he had worked without stopping, wheeling wounded soldiers in a wheelbarrow to the hospital sta-tions, for three days and the best part of three nights, and his shoulders had never straightened up again. He was the most powerful man I had ever seen. Once, he picked up a threshing hand who was foul-mouthing our family and carried him over his head to the back door of the carriage barn and threw him out on the manure pile. I admired him more than anyone I knew.

When I went up on the farmhouse porch he would come out and list the day's activities. Eugene Wills, the teamster, who lived in the cottage over the lawn, might be cultivating the cornfield with the sulky cultivator behind the grey team, or driving the mowing machine or the reaper, or plowing, according to the season. De Witt Parks, who lived in the farmhouse along with his son D-D, and who tended the poultry, would be clean-ing the hen house or fussing with the setting hens. He was a gaunt widower, too old for heavy work. D-D was already off with the spring wagon and the three great milk cans on his way to the cheese factory. Nelson him-self was doing chores around the barn because one of the registered heifers, Jacqueline De Koll, was about due with her first calf.

So it went, and I could make my plans for my day — where I wanted to be, and when. I didn't want to miss anything worth seeing; I felt more at home among the farm animals and poultry than I did in my own family; and in my way I found plenty to do. The cows went out to day pasture before I got up, but most days I went up over the uplands to find them and bring them back. And when the young turkeys got big enough, my brother and I would drive the whole flock of maybe two hundred up on the flats where they fed on grasshoppers all day among the sheep. The turkeys, though, always brought themselves home at sunset. They would take off at the steep edge of the flats and come sailing down through the sunset air to land at the edge of the creek. As my father got the notion of putting a sleigh bell around the necks of most of the old hens and gobblers, you could hear the silvery notes dropping down through the evening sky from all over the farm.

During the summer months, their only danger came from the larger hawks. But the turkeys took care of that in their own way. Each day four or five of the hens and gobblers would be posted as sentinels. They stayed in the outskirts of the flock, one eye or the other continually cocked sidewise at the sky till one wondered why they didn't get permanent neck cramps. The minute they spotted a hawk they would cluck and holler till the entire flock had been alerted. The hens would turn on their young ones, pecking and beating their wings to drive them under the nearest thorn-apple bush. With the young ones under the thorny branches, the hens would ring the bush facing out, while the gobblers strutted around the perimeter with hoarse, half-gobbling challenges. No hawk ever tried to break down those defenses. I think they might even have baffled a fox. Big turkeys are great fighters, and I once saw two hens jump an osprey who had lit on a young bird, shove him over on his back, and kill him right there, though it took quite a bit of time. Turkeys have a lot of knowledge in ways that suit themselves. And nights they were always in their own poultry house.

But with the guinea hens it was entirely different.

My father, who liked doing things in an impressive way, had decided to start his flock of guinea hens by buying three dozen birds. He thought they would add to the picturesque side of the farm, with their pale blue faces, red wattles, and speckled grey plumage. There was also in his mind the image of broiled young guinea hens appearing on a platter in front of him on the dining table. In the beginning it looked like a foolproof program. None of us, however, knew anything about their habits, if guinea hens can be said to have any habits at all.

They nested hit or miss, outdoors, wherever it fancied them to drop the first egg. I found most of these nests and marked them with a stake nearby fluttering a strip of red cotton, as a precaution against their not having hatched before the mowing started. Unfortunately, I did not find them all and we had casualties. But most did hatch out in good time, and after that we would see the adult birds whizzing up the drive in their strange, bent-forward run, or rushing through the barnyard, followed by a stream of tiny chicks like dark-brown mottled bumblebees. How the chicks ever managed to keep up was a mystery to everyone on the farm. The trouble was, however, that the adult birds were continually flying back and forth across the brook, and the babies, still in their soft down, had to swim as best they could with their little bare and stick-like feet. Nearly three-quarters of them, as far as we could tell, were drowned that way.

They had other irritating traits. They were always discussing with each other. You could hear their endless "pot-rack, pot-rack!" all over the place. When the young birds got old enough to stop peeping and "pot-rack" like their elders, the noise could be deafening. Along about midsummer they started coming over the brook and holding sunrise concourse on the front lawn, directly under my father's bedroom windows, and yelling there till he threw open the sash and began hurling sticks of firewood at them. This fazed them not at all. They merely withdrew from range and continued their clamor on a derisive note; and after three weeks, O'Toole, the coachman, whose duties included keeping the fireplaces stocked with wood, rebelled at bringing up another stick thrown out by no matter who, gave notice, and returned to the city.

So all of us learned to endure their rackety ways, and after my father stopped throwing wood out the window, they lost interest in our house and stayed mostly on the farm side of the brook.

August turned into September; the dark came earlier; the nights were cold enough for light upland frosts; and the tempo of the farm changed with the season. There were no grasshoppers left on the flats, and the turkeys stayed on the lower meadows. We no longer heard the cascade of sleigh bells as they planed down from the top of the hill. The dairy herd did not have to be hunted through the woods and glades at the back of the place; they would come winding down the sandy road at twilight of their own accord and wait at the gate at the foot of the hill, so that whoever fetched them had only two hundred yards to walk. The men going to the barn to milk carried lighted lanterns, which they hung above the runway between the rows of stanchions. The barn became a different place in lantern light, with the dust motes in the yellow air and only the rumps of the stanchioned cows clear to view, punctuated by the milkers and the soft slurring of the milk jets in the pails. You seemed to hear it much more clearly in the lantern light, with the big doors shut against the cold.

The early darkness also changed the nighttime habits of the poultry. The ducks clamored to get into the barn, where they had a pen in the hall-like space that separated the cowbarn from the horses' stable at the far end. The hens entered their house earlier than before, rooting around the chaff floor for the cracked corn and hopping sleepily to the roosting board as the shadows thickened. The turkey flock, depleted now by the sale of most of the young birds for broilers, were glad to go into their own house beyond the hog house on what was called the hog-house hill. But the biggest change took place among the guinea hens. All summer they had moved about in high independence of each other, perching anywhere their fancy struck them or squatting in a tuft of grass. Now all at once they joined in a single flock and every night marched in formation, in what was almost a parading of the guard, through the farm buildings and up the hog-house hill to a large black-cherry tree, on whose wide limbs they roosted in long lines. When the great, full October moon rose

over the pond we could see their bumpy silhouettes
stuck tight to the spreading branches.

The mornings too were slower to get started. I
would hear the herd bells moving off along the road to
day pasture as I was getting dressed, while in summer
they were often gone before I woke. The routine of the
farm seemed to contract, as if in preparation for the
harsh constriction of our northern winter. Frost was
not only on the uplands now; it crackled in the grass
when I went out after breakfast, and if I walked up to
the dam, as I often did, I could see the frost mists rising
off the water, forming swaying pillars of white, like
ghosts fading before day.

I was coming back from the dam one morning when
I saw the first of the strange tubelike objects that mysti-
fied not only myself but everyone else on the place. It
was about an inch and a half long and a quarter inch in
diameter. I thought it was a worm, but when I picked
it up it was rubbery and harder than a worm would be,
and its ends were square, as if cut by a knife. Then I
noticed a speckled grey guinea feather, and after a
moment came on three more beyond it. But I saw no
reason to connect them with the little pink tube.

Nor did my father, when I showed it to him. He
didn't seem much interested. Nobody was. It was just
one of those things that continually turned up on any
farm. No one knew what it was, and it didn't matter,
because you'd never see another. But the next morning
I found another one, very nearly in the same spot. This
time a lot of feathers were lying about, and it seemed
obvious that something drastic had happened to a
guinea hen there.

I brought the little piece of tubing back to the house and this time it aroused more interest and speculation; but nobody knew what it was. In my own mind I felt that something evil and terrible was coming out of the autumn woods after dark, and now De Witt Parks, the poultryman, came to my father and said that he felt sure that something was getting at the guinea hens. He had found feathers for two nights under the cherry tree they roosted on, and to make sure, he had picked all the feathers up the night before, but this morning there had been a new batch of them.

For two days I found no more pink tubes. Then on the third day there was another up on the dam. I picked it up as I had the others. The dam was white with frost that morning, my feet had left plain black prints in it, and I realized that around the spot where I had picked up the tube, there was no other track. Whatever was responsible might have come early in the night, I supposed, and the frost fell heaviest towards morning, covering tracks. But that did not seem likely to me.

I went back to the house again with my find, but my father was busy talking to an old man he sometimes went hunting with. Birdy Morris had come around to see if Father would go off for an afternoon of partridge shooting and hoped also to arrange a deer-hunting party for next Sunday if Father would agree to let them hunt our land or, better yet, to join their party.

I could see them discussing this while I stood looking in through the living-room window, and presently Birdy caught my eye. I heard him say, "Your boy out there looks as if he wanted to see us."

"Oh, yes," my father said. "He's been finding some peculiar things around the place. He's probably found another."

They called me in and I showed the small pink piece of tubing to Birdy. He was a shortish man who looked even shorter because one shoulder was deformed. But his eyes were bright as the eyes of a wild thing peering from a thicket. He took the tubing from me and rolled it gently between thumb and finger.

"Yes," he said. "It's a piece of something's windpipe. Can't say what, with just it to look at."

"There were some guinea feathers," I said.

"That's it, then. You've got an owl raiding your guinea hens. Horn owl, it will be. That's how they kill. Two claws and cut a piece out of the windpipe clean as razors."

He went on to say that the horn owl wasn't afraid of anything that he had ever heard of. (Father later said that Birdy Morris should have called it a great horned owl; but you couldn't expect a backwoods type like him to know such things.) They were bigger than the barred owls and a tarnation sight more powerful. They'd go for just about anything. One once had gone for him.

"Got into my attic loft through a broke window. My wife — she was alive then — kept telling me to mend it, but you know how them things be. I heard a noise up there and went up through the trapdoor and the danged thing hit me. Lucky I had my hat on and he took that. You can bet I had the door shut before he found it wasn't me, and the next time I opened it I had my scatter gun poked through ahead of me."

Abruptly, as old men will, he lost interest in me and owls and turned to finish his business with my father. When I went out across the brook to tell Nelson and De Witt what Birdy had told us, I saw his bent-shouldered figure ambling down the river road.

I showed the windpipe to Nelson, who said he had never heard of such a thing, but was inclined to believe it, if Birdy said so. Birdy knew everything there was to know about the woods and the animals who lived among them. De Witt was skeptical. It did not seem a rational way for anything, wild or not, to kill some other thing. He was busy anyway giving the hen house its monthly cleanup and scattering the first winter layer of chaff over the floor.

But that afternoon, just before sundown, he came over the brook to talk to my father.

"There's something funny going on with the guinea hens," he said. "They're standing under that cherry tree they roost on but there's not one flown up into it. They're all hollering and yelling. Seems almost they're hollering by turns."

Father told De Witt not to worry about it. In his opinion all the guinea hens were crazy.

De Witt shook his head. "Seems almost as if they wasn't going to roost there tonight, and they're trying to make up their minds where to go to instead."

"They haven't got any minds," my father said impatiently. "Forget about them, De Witt."

But De Witt wasn't satisfied. And sure enough, when I went out with him to the barnyard, we saw the guinea hens coming down off the hog-house hill. They moved in close order at their usual running gait, whizzing around the corner of the big cowbarn and heading straight for the hen house.

"Just as if they knowed where they was going," De Witt said admiringly.

They obviously did know, for as they reached the hen-yard fence, the leading birds turned to face the rest of the flock. There was a brief, intense harangue. Then the leaders flew up and over the fence, followed in threes and fours by the rest. Inside the yard they formed up close and marched on the three small poultry openings that led into the house, running up the sloping boards that led to them and into the hen house. A moment later there was a protesting outcry from the hens. When De Witt and I looked through the door the hens were standing in a huddle on the floor, still protesting, and the guinea hens had taken over the roost.

"What you going to do with them?" I asked.

"Nothing," De Witt said. "If we tried to get them out now, there'd be such a commotion the hens wouldn't come back into the house for a week, let alone lay an egg. You don't ever want any commotion around hens if you can help it. Their minds addle too easy." He took his hat off in order to scratch the top of his head. "Maybe Birdy Morris is right," he allowed. "And if it's an owl, I want to do something about getting rid of it. Come on, we'll go see your pa again."

We went back to the big house and found my father in the living room. De Witt told him about the guinea hens. "I can't get rid of them tonight, but I'll close the chicken doors tomorrow before they get down there.

But Mr. Edmonds, we ought to take care of that owl, or whatever it is, before he goes after something else."

"What do you suggest, De Witt?"

"I want to take a Plymouth Rock pullet and wire her to a limb of that cherry tree and set a trap."

"Seems a shame to waste a pullet that way," my father said. "But go ahead if you think you can catch the owl."

So we went back across the brook, and while De Witt went to get a pullet, I hunted out Nelson and asked for an Oneida jump trap. Then I went up to the cherry tree on the hog-house hill.

De Witt was already there with a dead pullet and some fine wire. The bottom branch, which a large part of the guinea hen flock had used for roosting, was within his reach. He wired the body of the pullet to it and in what I considered an artful way. It rested breast down on the branch, and he had tucked its head underneath a wing. It looked for all the world like a pullet sleeping on its roost. Then he set the trap and with a piece of heavy thread tied it on the back of the dead pullet, passed the chain around the branch, and stapled the ring at the end of it solidly into the wood.

"I don't expect a bird's knowing about traps, like a fox or mink," De Witt said, as we walked back down the hill to the barn. "But we'll see in the morning."

As we were sitting at breakfast next morning a great to-do of gasping exclamations broke out in the kitchen, and Maggie, the waitress, hurried in to tell my father that De Witt had something to show him.

"Tell him to come in," my father said, and a moment later De Witt's gaunt, bony figure edged in through the pantry door. He was wearing Eugene the teamster's heaviest leather gloves and holding the legs of a great owl whose body was tucked under his arm.

I remember as if it were today the way the great bird looked, his golden eyes glaring at us, the tufts that got him his name of "horned" erect and stiff. Beneath De Witt's gloved hands the thickly feathered toes with their curved talons opened and closed. He may have been afraid but all I remember in his face was his scorn and hatred for us all. If he felt any fear, he did not let it show.

My mother turned quite pale. "Oh, De Witt," she said, "how dreadful!" And De Witt, who obviously did not think it was dreadful at all, said, "Yes, mam."

"What are you going to do with him?" Father asked.

"I have a chicken crate for him in Nelson's cellar," De Witt replied. "We can't let him go."

"No. Will he eat anything?" my father asked.

"We haven't tried," said De Witt.

"Well, put him back in it," my father said, "and we'll decide what to do."

De Witt took him away. Asking to be excused, I followed him. There was the same flutter among the maids. The cook thought the owl looked "fearful," but the waitress exclaimed, "Oh, no! He's beautiful. See the golden eyes on him!" Both of them seemed rather ridiculous to me, and I walked out behind De Witt and over the brook to the open bulkhead doors leading down into Nelson's cellar. Only two of the high, small windows in the foundation wall were open to the sky, and the cellar was dark enough for my eyes to take a minute to adjust themselves. Then I could see De Witt kneeling before a chicken crate, which for some reason was on its side, against the far wall. I could not think why until, with infinite carefulness to avoid the owl's beak, he maneuvered the bird through the door. The owl still snapped his beak at him through the bars of the crate; it made a thin, brittle, almost pathetically small sound, but its fierceness was unmistakable.

De Witt stood up and then I could see why the crate was on its side. Unless it had been, the owl could not have stood upright. As we drew back he seemed to compose himself. His wings, which had been spread an inch or two away from his body as he threatened De Witt through the bars of the crate, now closed. The owl stood perfectly still but his ferocity remained undiminished. As I turned to follow De Witt up the bulkhead steps I felt the bird's eyes staring after me. Even when I had closed the bulkhead doors I seemed to see them.

At noon there was another stir in the kitchen. The waitress had gone to see the owl in Nelson's cellar and, putting her hand too close to the crate, had had a piece taken out of the end of her finger.

"He'll have to be killed," my father said.

But that evening De Witt and Nelson came over to our house. De Witt carried the owl by its legs, barehanded. The bird hung inert, his wings limply spread. He had died of natural causes, Nelson and De Witt decided. If confinement in a chicken crate in a farmhouse cellar, with the stamp of people walking overhead, can be considered natural for an owl, maybe they were right. But it seemed to me that he had died of hatred and the dread he did not let us see.

SC
E

Edmonds, Walter D.

The night raider and
other stories

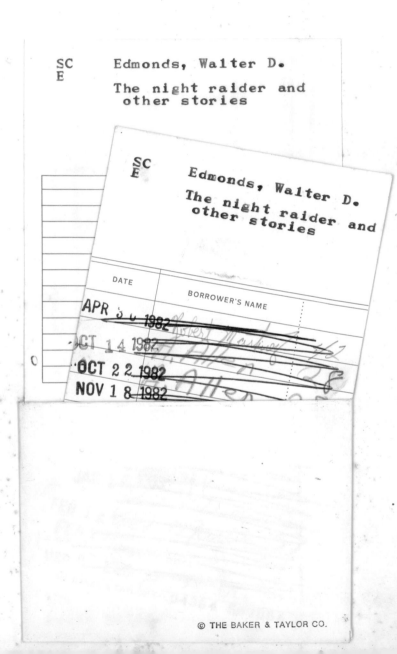

SC
E

Edmonds, Walter D.

The night raider and
other stories

DATE	BORROWER'S NAME
APR 3 0 1982	
OCT 1 4 1982	
OCT 2 2 1982	
NOV 1 8 1982	